I0767819

IRISH ROSE ORPHANS' CHRISTMAS

Prequel to Irish Rose Orphans:

A Thousand Islands Gilded Age Series

by
Susan G Mathis

smWordWorks llc
Fiction

Irish Rose Orphans' Christmas

Prequel to Irish Rose Orphans: A Thousand Islands Gilded Age Series by Susan G Mathis
Published by smWordWorks, llc

ISBN-13: 979-8-9876796-2-3

Editor: Denise Farnsworth

Available in print and e-book. For more information visit:
www.SusanGMathis.com/fiction

Visit her at www.SusanGMathis.com

Sign up for her newsletter

and please consider writing an Amazon review. Thanks!

DEDICATION

To my four granddaughters, Reagan, Madison, Devyn, and Peyton, who inspired these wonderful characters.

To my son, daughter, and son-in-law, who have always encouraged my writing. I am grateful for family.

To the Thousand Islands River Rats and especially to my faithful readers who love the river as much as I do. Thanks for your support in reading my stories, sharing them with others, and writing reviews on Amazon and Barnes & Noble. You bless me.

ACKNOWLEDGMENTS

I hope you enjoy *Irish Rose Orphans' Christmas, the Prequel to Irish Rose Orphans: A Thousand Islands Gilded Age Series.* If you've read any of my other books, you know that I love introducing history to my readers through fictional stories.

This story is a little different, introducing seven orphans who live in an orphanage in Brooklyn as they prepare to go into service as teens. Then, the series will follow the journey of the different girls a decade later as they go to the Thousand Islands as servants for various Gilded Age island owners. These young women serve on islands such as Friendly Island, Comfort Island, Nobby Island, St. Elmo Island, and more. Please note that I took a bit of creative license in bringing this story to life, so some of the timing is a little different than recorded.

Thanks to you, my readers, for your faithful support and for staying connected. I love hearing from you. And a special thanks …

To Judy Keeler, my wonderful historical editor, who combs through my manuscripts for accuracy. Because of her, you can trust that my stories are historically correct.

To my fabulous Beta Team, Barb, Donna, Melinda, and Laurie, who inspire me with your kindness, faithfulness, and wisdom. You are dear friends and a precious team.

To my amazing editor, Denise Farnsworth, for sharing your amazing talents with me.

And to all my dear friends who have journeyed with me in my writing. Thanks for your emails, social media posts, and especially for your reviews. Most of all, thanks for your friendship.

And to God, from whom all good gifts come. Without You, there would never be a dream of writing what I do or the ability to fulfill that dream.

CAST OF CHARACTERS

Brooklyn 1876

Seven orphaned girls, on the cusp of womanhood, prepare for a life of service beyond the asylum's walls. Bound by faith and friendship, they face a Christmas of parting that will test their hearts and forge their futures.

~ ~ ~

Annie Burns (Age 14)

Warm-hearted and impulsive, Annie is eager to please but often avoids conflict, unlike her twin sister, Taryn. Scatterbrained and tender, she hides her fears behind acts of devotion. She's training to be a lady's maid under Sister Agnes, a former lady's maid herself.

Taryn Burns (Age 14)

Annie's twin sister. Intelligent and serious, Taryn's heart is walled off by bitterness and distrust. A perfectionist, she masks her pain with cynicism and precision. She's a nurse-in-training under Sister Clare, the convent's gardener and healer.

Fiona King (Age 16)

Quiet and fiercely independent, Fiona observes more than she speaks. Her strength and intensity make her a natural protector, though shame and resentment toward authority shadow her spirit. She's assistant cook to Sister Bernadette, the novice nun who oversees the kitchen.

Isabel Sweeney (Age 14)

Poised and private, Isabel commands respect with her calm confidence. Her steady nature makes her the group's anchor, especially for her younger sister, Gloria, though her need for control sometimes isolates her. She the secretary-in-training under Sister Rose, the headmistress.

Gloria Sweeney (Age 13)

Isabel's younger sister, Gloria is sensitive and intuitive. She feels deeply and loves fiercely. Her compassion and wisdom set her apart, but fear and envy often cloud her gentle heart. She's training to be a lady's maid under Sister Agnes and a gifted singer.

Vivian Dunne (Age 15)

Outspoken and brave, Vivian leads the girls with humor and courage. She's creative and resilient, using laughter to mask the ache of feeling she'll never quite belong. Vivian is a nanny-in-training with the youngest orphan girls.

Cassie Mulberry (Age 15)

Studious and disciplined, Cassie approaches life like a ledger—balanced, efficient, and exact. Her intelligence earns respect, though her sharp tongue and self-assurance keep others at arm's length. She's a bookkeeper-in-training under Sister Rose.

~ ~ ~

The Sisters of the Irish Rose

Sister Rose Donnelly – Headmistress

Oversees the asylum's operations, admissions, and spiritual care. Wise and compassionate, she guides each girl toward her calling, offering grace even when others offer judgment.

Sister Agnes – Household Supervisor

A former lady's maid, she manages daily routines and moral discipline. Stern but fair, she believes order is the highest kindness.

Sister Clare – Caretaker and Infirmarian

Tends the girls' ailments with herbs, prayer, and gentle wisdom. Her garden is both sanctuary and schoolroom for Taryn and others who seek healing.

Sister Catherine – Head Teacher

A strict disciplinarian who values obedience above mercy. Her sharp words wound more deeply than she knows.

Sister Bernadette – Kitchen and Laundry Supervisor
Kind but overburdened, she teaches through service. In her warm kitchen, the girls learn not only to cook, but to find joy in humble tasks.

CHAPTER 1

December 3, 1876 – Brooklyn, New York

The snow had fallen overnight like a whisper, cushioning the edges of the city, hiding the grime beneath a hush of white. Outside the frosty windows of the Irish Rose Orphan Asylum for Girls, Brooklyn stirred under its first snowfall, horses' hooves muffled beneath sleigh runners and chimney smoke curled like prayers into the cotton-ball sky. It should have been peaceful. But inside Annie's chest, a different kind of storm was gathering.

From the second-floor dormitory window, Annie Burns watched the world transform—carriage wheels making muddy tracks, boys with ash-pale faces hurling snowballs in the street, and the steeples of the nearby church gleaming. It reminded her of a Christmas card like Sister Rose might tuck into her Bible for her to cherish forever.

Yet inside the only house that ever felt like home since she'd lost her parents, everything was cold, dark, and heavy. She traced a circle on the frost- glazed glass, her breath forming a cloud, then fading. Just like everything else in her life.

Taryn's bed sat made across the room, tucked with military precision. Not a wrinkle in sight. That's how she was. Always buttoned-up, polished, and impenetrable. It was how Annie's twin existed these days.

Yet her own bed was a tangle of quilts and books and a half-darned stocking she didn't care to finish. Their whole life had become like this— separate corners and separate selves.

Annie sighed, a tear slipping out of her eye unbidden. It used to be so different. When they were small, they'd curled up under the same covers, whispering secrets and stories into the dark. They'd shared everything. The same womb. The same birthday, and the same deep chestnut-brown curls. The same hazel-green eyes, though her twin's were darker.

Three years ago, she and her sister had clung to each other through the first bleak winter at Irish Rose, when everything had smelled like vinegar and boiled cabbage and the only way to sleep was to pretend Papa hadn't left and Mama didn't flee to life beyond the pearly gates when they were just six. Then, after five years under Uncle Milton's care, he'd died, joining Mama—leaving them to be all alone in an orphanage.

Now Taryn and she barely spoke to each other. The worst part? She couldn't put her finger on the moment their relationship broke.

Was it last Christmas, when she had corrected Taryn in front of Sister Agnes? Or the time Taryn had refused to sneak bread to one of the younger girls because it was "against the rules," and Annie scoffed?

Maybe it had started when Annie told her twin she didn't want to be a servant or a nurse, that she wanted to be more, and Taryn had just stared at her as though she was lazy or crazy or lost. Most likely, though, Taryn was still mad that Annie had been adopted for those two short years and had left Taryn behind.

Annie slammed the shutters closed and turned away. She couldn't be late for the special meeting Sister Rose had summoned the seven older girls to attend.

She hurried downstairs and stood in the hallway outside the chapel, clutching her shawl against the chill. The shawl had once belonged to her mother—at least, that's what Sister Agnes had told her long ago, and whether it was true or not didn't matter much now. It was the only thing left of her mother.

"Are you coming in or just planning to stand in the hallway, Willow?" a familiar sound teased behind her.

Annie didn't turn, but she knew it was Vivian—the boldest, the loudest, the one who called herself "Captain" and half the time acted as though she ran the place. Despite herself, Annie smiled. "I'm thinking about the days to come."

Vivian huffed. "Thinkin' can get you in trouble." Annie glanced at her over her shoulder. "And I'm sure that you never think about your tomorrows." Vivian grinned, mischief dancing in her eyes.

But when Annie didn't laugh, Vivian's smile dimmed, and she touched Annie's arm in a rare moment of gentleness. "Come. They're waiting for us."

Vivian disappeared through the heavy oak doors, and Annie followed, the chapel warm and dim, the air thick with beeswax and cedar oil. The girls sat scattered across the pews, but the silence between herself and Taryn hung in the air while the others stoically waited.

She took her seat two rows behind her twin. Alone.

Taryn sat with her back straight, her chestnut braid twisted tight like a crown, not one hair out of place. Annie stared at her perfect coiffure, fists clenched in her lap. She used to braid that chestnut hair every night until her fingers knew each strand by heart. Now she could scarcely look at her beloved sister without wanting to scream as she smoothed her own tousled braids.

Annie scanned the room as they waited for the meeting to start. Vivian squirmed as if she wanted to hop up and shout. Fiona knelt at the front as though the world sat on her shoulders. Isabel and Gloria sat side by side, their fingers entwined like lifelines. Cassie scribbled in her little notebook as though truth could be captured in ink.

Sister Rose stood before them, framed by the unlit Advent wreath, her countenance calm. "This year, we will prepare not just for Christ's coming but for your going. But before you leave us, you must get ready for what is to come by searching your hearts." Her gaze rested on each girl like a gentle blessing. "What truths do you need to face? What heartache still haunts you? What burdens must you leave behind?"

Annie bit her lip so hard she tasted blood.

As instructed, Fiona solemnly lit the first candle in the Advent wreath, the hope candle, with trembling hands, Sister Rose prayed and invited them to sit in stillness or light a votive when they were ready. Gloria wiped her eyes, and Cassie nibbled on her pencil deep in thought. Vivian cracked a half-hearted joke. Taryn scooted past Cassie and left through the side door.

Annie stood. She didn't want to stay and pretend she was peaceful, not tonight. She fled the solemn scene, refusing to feel or think.

Outside the chapel, the hallway was empty. She rounded the corner to step outside for some air, and there was Taryn, arms folded tightly around her middle.

"Are you following me? You needn't bother." Taryn's hazel eyes blazed as she folded her arms. Her words were cool but not angry. Worse— dismissive. Annie stopped short. "Don't start."

"I'm not starting anything. But Sister Rose asked us to face truth, to prepare for—"

"For what?" Annie snapped, louder than she meant. "For being sent away like we're parcels on a train? For saying goodbye to everyone and pretending it doesn't tear us apart? Blathers, sister."
Taryn blinked, a reflection of her own.

Annie's chest heaved. "You seem just fine with it. As though none of it matters." Frustration simmered just below the surface. "You sit in there with your straight back and your perfect answers and act like everything's under control, like you don't feel anything."

"Nae, I do feel things, Annie." Taryn shook her head, her words clipped. "I just don't fall apart every time something changes."

Annie flinched when the words hit her like slaps. "Is that what you think I am? Falling apart?" "I think you don't know what you want, and it terrifies you."

Taryn narrowed her eyes, glaring at her. "You want to be close to me, Annie, but then you push me away. You want us to talk, but then you hurry off. You're annoyed with me, but you say nothing, and I can't fix it. I'm your sister, not your scapegoat."

Silence fell between them, and Annie swallowed hard. "I don't need you to solve things, Taryn, I just want you to understand."

Taryn's expression relaxed, just a little. "I do understand. You think I don't feel scared too? That the gulf between us doesn't hurt, or that I don't lie awake at night wondering who I'll be when I'm not part of us anymore?"

That pierced Annie deep in her heart. She looked down at her trembling hands. "I'm afraid you'll forget me."

Taryn stepped closer, maintaining control. "Annie, no matter what happens, I will never forget you."

The hush that followed wasn't cold anymore. It was fragile and honest, like the first light through storm clouds.

"We can't fix it all today." Taryn's clipped and guarded tone lifted a little. "But maybe…we could talk, really talk, when you're ready."

Annie nodded, forcing a slight smile. "I'd like that."

Taryn nodded, walked away, and slipped through the heavy chapel door without another word. She barely acknowledged Annie's agreement to talk, and they didn't hug. But as Annie turned to go back into the chapel, the ache inside her loosened just a little, like a tight knot beginning to untie.

She reentered the dimly lit room as she searched for her twin. Taryn sat a few pews from the back, her profile tight. The same stubborn jaw. She'd maintain her unceasing control no matter what.

Yet Annie chose to believe a fragile string of hope still dangled between them.

She took a seat in the last pew—on the edge of the group but not quite apart. How had the rift between her twin and herself grown wider and deeper, ever since she'd left Taryn at the orphanage when she was adopted? It had to be more, and it wasn't just about leaving the Irish Rose.

Sister Rose waited by the altar, the Advent wreath on it with its one lit candle. When she spoke, the room stilled. "As you know, the seven of you will soon be going out into the world to find your purpose, to find out what God has planned for you."

A shiver ran through Annie—not from the cold, but from the truth she knew, though none of them had ever spoken aloud. After the New Year, they would be sent out—into homes not their own, to serve families they'd never met. Some as housemaids, some as governesses, and some, like Taryn, as nurses, or others like Fiona, a cook. All of them scattered like seed on the wind. And herself? That was a fearsome mystery yet to be solved.

"I know this Christmas is your last together in this house." The gentle tone in Sister Rose's words drew tears to Annie's eyes, and, she suspected, to a few others too. Probably not to Taryn's. "So, I ask you to enter into this Advent with open hearts. Let God speak to the places in you that are hurting, to the places that are afraid, and to the places that need the light of hope or peace. And let this season rekindle joy and love deep inside you so that you can take it with you for the rest of your lives."

Annie's throat tightened. She didn't want to go. Not yet.

"Each Sunday before Christmas, we will light a candle. The candles will represent something you will need for the road ahead. Hope. Peace. Joy. And love."

Sister Rose smiled. "But we must begin with facing your past. What burdens are you carrying, my daughters? What offenses do you need to release into His hands? What sorrows must you lay down before the Christ child?"

Annie glanced at her friends. Fiona lowered her auburn head, and Isabel's graceful shoulders trembled. Even Vivian's brave grin faded.

But Annie couldn't pray. Her burden had no label—only the ache of her sister sitting just a few feet away, still miles apart.

After the closing prayer, the girls dispersed, reluctant to leave the warmth of the candles or the safety of Sister Rose. Annie stood and turned to go but froze as she nearly collided with Taryn.

For a moment, they just looked at each other. A flicker passed between them—familiar, aching, and full of something lost.

Taryn broke the tension first. "That shawl is going to tear if you keep holding it so tight."

Annie sighed. "Then maybe it matches me." She hadn't meant to say it, but the words slipped out like breath on frosty glass.

Taryn's mouth opened, then closed. She stepped aside without another word, urging Annie onward.

Annie walked past her, her heart pounding and throat thick with regret. One step forward, two steps back. It was always that way with her sister. How could she break through this wall or traverse this chasm? What was it, really? She couldn't even name it, and that frustrated her the most. At least, if she knew what it was, then she could try to settle it or speak to it and try to solve it. But without knowing what it was, she could do nothing.

She entered the hallway alone, the girls having scattered, so she stood at the window to think. Outside, the snow had stopped. The first candle of Advent had been lit. But in Annie's chest, a different kind of fire flickered.

Could she find truth in her twin breach? Could she tear down the wall between Taryn and herself? She had to try.

Hope. That was the first candle. She'd grasp onto it with all her might.

Maybe there was still time to find it.

CHAPTER 2

Late that evening, Taryn padded to the chapel, lit the hope candle, and lingered there for what felt like hours. She had to think. Alone.

She'd spent most of her life trying not to feel too much. It was safer and neater that way, for emotions were like spilled ink. Once they bled through the page, they were impossible to hide. So, she kept everything in order—her bed made, her shoes polished, and her prayers memorized and said on time. She was the dependable one, the composed one, the twin who didn't blubber when their parents vanished from their lives like mist. But tonight, her throat ached with the pressure of everything she'd kept inside.

The hope candle flickered on the Advent wreath. Sister Rose's words lingered like incense. "What burden must you stop carrying alone?"

Taryn didn't even know where to begin. Annie's plea still rang in her ears—sharp, aching, and too raw to ignore. "I just want you to understand."

"I do understand," she'd said, and it was true. She saw Annie's disappointment and grief, though she never looked her straight in the eye, and her own unconfessed pain swirled through her. But what Annie didn't see—what none of them saw—was how hard Taryn had to work not to fall apart too. If she let go…who would be left to hold Annie and the others up?

The hallway was dark by the time Taryn blew out the candle and stepped out of the chapel, the hush pressing in like a ghost. She shuffled to the dormitory, her hands curled into fists in her coat pockets. She expected Annie to be asleep like the others, buried under her quilt, and her back turned, but her twin's bed was empty.

The memory of their conversation still rang in her ears. "You want us to talk, but then you storm off…You think I don't feel scared too?"

She hadn't meant to let that truth slip, but Annie always had a way of digging past her defenses. Maybe because they shared the same face, the same past, and the same pain, just buried differently.

She had built her whole self around not admitting weakness, especially after Annie didn't fight for them to stay together when Annie was the only one chosen to be a part of a family for those two terrible years. At least, terrible for Taryn.

She walked to the window and looked out. The courtyard appeared gray under the moonlight, the snow coating the bushes like icing. But a small movement caught her eye. Someone sat, curled on the bench, beneath the arbor.

Annie. Of course. She'd know that willowy shape anywhere.

She grabbed a shawl and crept downstairs, the stone steps seeping cold through her boots. Outside, the air bit at her skin. Annie sat motionless, her arms wrapped around her knees, staring up at the stars as though she searched for answers.

Taryn approached her sister. "Goodness, Annie! You'll freeze out here."

Annie didn't look at her. "Wouldn't be the worst thing."

She took a seat beside Annie, draping the shawl across both their shoulders. They sat in stillness for a while, but the closeness warming something deeper than skin. "I'm sorry."

Annie looked to the heavens and blinked. "For what?"

"For forgetting that being strong doesn't mean being silent."

Her twin turned toward her. "You've been strong for both of us for a long time."

Taryn nodded, her jaw tight. "But sometimes it feels as though you don't care, so I've built a wall to hold everything in, and now I don't know how to tear it down."

"You don't have to do it all at once," Annie said, gentler than she'd sounded in weeks. "Maybe just…let me sit on the other side of the wall for a bit. Remember the Irish proverb Papa used to say, 'Making the beginning is one-third of the work.'"

Taryn laughed—just a tiny whisper of it, unguarded and surprised. "That sounds like something Papa would say."

"He was always spouting such sayings." The corner of Annie's mouth lifted in agreement.

Taryn's eyes stung, and she looked away. "You know…I'm scared too. Of what happens next and being sent out. Of who I'll have to become to survive as I did the last time."

"You don't have to become anything but you," Annie implored. "Even if we're in different houses or states or—" She stopped, her voice cracking. "Even then, we're still us. Twins and sisters. Always."

A sacred awe followed. A gentle hush against the years of separation. A truce from the silent war.
"I miss you," Taryn whispered.

Annie leaned her head against Taryn's shoulder. "Then come back to me."

Taryn pursed her lips, the wind biting at her cheeks. It was too much, too fast. Suddenly, she pulled away, the shawl slipping from her shoulders like a weight she wasn't ready to share. She couldn't do this, for if she jumped over that chasm and fell into it, she might not survive.

Annie shifted beside her. "What is it?"

Taryn couldn't answer at first. The words were there, crowding her throat and crashing against the dam she'd built. She stood, her arms crossed against the cold—and against her sister. "I shouldn't have come. This was…a mistake."

Annie looked up, confused and hurt. "You said you missed me."

"I do." Her words cracked, then hardened. "But missing you doesn't change anything." She turned away, blinking into the dark and willing the stars to blur so she wouldn't have to admit how close she was to crying. Too much had cracked open, and she didn't know how to put it back together. She swiped her tears away.

Annie watched her—she could feel her eyes boring into her back seeing too much as always. And perhaps that was the problem.

"I don't know how to do this," Taryn implored, turning around to face her. "I don't know how to be close to you or vulnerable. I used to think I was being strong, but now…" She trailed off. "Now it feels as though I'm standing weaponless on a battlefield."

"You don't have to be perfect, Taryn," Annie offered.

"Oh, but I do." Her tone sharpened. "You don't understand. When I mess up, people don't forgive me. They file reports, and they move me. They call it progress when, really, it's just the exile of someone who's failed."

She didn't mean to say that much. A long pause stretched between them, brittle and aching. Annie reached for her again, but Taryn stepped back, shaking her head.

"Nae. If I let myself believe things could go back to how they were…" she paused, swallowing her angst.

"And if they don't, I can't survive another fracture. Not from you."

Annie's hazel eyes glistened in the moonlight breaking through the clouds. "So, you'd rather walk away now than risk being hurt?"

"Yes." The word came out too fast and final. But it was the only thing safe and real. Taryn turned and fled her twin's presence, the night swallowing her footsteps. She wasn't a bad sister. She was just tired of pretending that hope didn't cost too much.

Behind her, Annie didn't call out, and Taryn told herself that was good. Silence granted her protection, and walking away meant strength. She couldn't let herself lean into the awful feelings she'd clung to for so long, so she ran away from the pain— and the tenderness. That terrible twin-shaped hole in her heart.

But deep down, an inner voice whispered— You're not building walls anymore. You're digging a grave.

The cold stung worse once she left Annie behind. Each step away from her pricked Taryn's skin like icicles, but she didn't stop. If she turned around now, she'd unravel right there in the snow.

She kept retreating until the only light was the gleam of the stars and the faint orange glow of the fire through the orphanage window behind frosted glass. She crouched behind the woodshed, tucked her arms around her knees, and let herself moan—a ragged and angry sound.

Why did I say all that?

The worst part wasn't walking away—it was how much she wanted Annie to follow. She wanted Annie to argue and pull her back, and say she wasn't too broken or too hardened to be loved. She wanted her twin to chase her down and tell her she mattered.

But Annie hadn't, for her sister never followed or fussed. She never fought for her.

Boundaries and distance meant safety, right? The hollow space inside her screamed louder than logic. It echoed with memories she hadn't invited— as wee sisters, the two of them giggling together. Annie braiding her hair with fingers that fumbled but always tried.

Precious late nights with whispered sister secrets under shared blankets.

All of that distant now. All of it out of reach.

You're not the sister Annie remembers, she thought bitterly. You're the version who learned to build walls and keep quiet to survive. The one who learned how to shrink without being told and who cries when no one is watching.

But she hated this version of herself, and it was the only one that remained.

She leaned her forehead to her knees. The night was so still, it was as if the earth had paused to witness her breaking.

The thing was—she hadn't lied to Annie. She was scared of what came next and of being placed again in a terrible, awful situation, and of letting someone into her heart just long enough for them to leave.

She wanted to be held and be seen. No, she wanted to scream!

But all she did was sit there, curled into herself like a secret, wishing she could be someone else.

Someone braver and less like a stiff, cold, wintery gale that had forgotten how to cease its fury.

The snow came steady now, as if the world were trying to muffle her pain with a blanket she hadn't asked for.

Still, she didn't move. She sat there for what could've been minutes or hours, numb in body but afflicted in mind—trapped in the cage of her own thoughts.

You always leave before they can leave you. That was her rule she had never spoken aloud but followed like gospel.

Cassie had said once, "You push people away so you don't have to watch them choose someone else."

Taryn had laughed it off and said something sarcastic. But Cassie looked at her with that all- knowing look, and maybe she'd been right.

She longed for a sign, a reason to believe she still mattered. But maybe she didn't.

You don't get to be the victim, she reminded herself. You're the one who walks away.

Her chest ached—a deep, dull throb like a nasty bruise beneath the surface—the kind of ache that returned when you thought you were fine, and after you'd told everyone you were fine.

She rested her head back against the shed wall, feeling the icy cold creep through the fabric of her shawl. Her breath rose in pale clouds, vanishing before they reached the stars.

What if Annie had had enough? What if this time, there wasn't a solution? No more shared blanket or whispered reassurances. No more "we'll figure it out together."

What if the bond she kept trying to protect by retreating…was already broken?

She clenched her fists. She hated how much caring still made her feel as though she was cracking open. It hurt that love and grief came tangled together like ivy she couldn't rip free of without tearing something vital underneath.

You don't get to fall apart, she told herself again. You're the strong one. The one who doesn't cry. The one who holds the line so no one else has to.

But in the dark, with no one watching, she let her tears fall—controlled like a confession. Not sobs or loud. More like a gradual leaking of all the things she couldn't say, all the things she still carried—the fear, the shame, the desperate wish to be small and safe again—and be enough.

She didn't know how long she cried. Just that when the tears stopped, the ache didn't. And all she was left with was brokenness.

CHAPTER 3

Vivian Dunne was not about to let her Irish Rose sisters fall into mopey melancholy—not on her watch. She had to change the mood, and fast. It had been two tense days of emotions.

The twins were sniping again, tossing barbs sharp enough to slice bread. Vivian didn't care what it was this time—something about a lost ribbon or who called who selfish. Why, those two would fight about a gnat if they saw one land near them these days. What mattered was that the tension was thick as porridge and just as depressing.

Their placements were days away. Everyone was twitchy, thin-skinned, and nervous. Even Cassie, the most unshakeable of the lot, looked as though she might cry or bite someone. Maybe both.

Well, this life wasn't so bad, especially after losing her parents in a tenement fire at age six and being passed between orphanages and workhouses until she arrived at the Irish Rose at age nine. Here, for the first time, she was seen. And these girls needed to stop being so sad and shake off their morbs.

Vivian couldn't stand it. "Let's move, girls! In two shakes of a lamb's tail," she hollered, hands on her hips like a miniature general. "Charades! Winner gets one of the caramels Sister Clare hides in her drawer like it's one of the crown jewels!"

A few girls blinked at her. Isabel muttered something snarky, but Vivian didn't care—she was already in mid-performance, marching across the common room with her face twisted into a thundercloud.

"Guess who I am." She growled, her chin tucked as though she'd swallowed vinegar. She swiped at a wild curl. "Hint—it's a rotten bit of luck when you're around her."

"Sister Catherine!" someone shouted.

Vivian grinned wide enough to flash both dimples. "Ten points to the clever lass in the corner!"

The atmosphere of the room shifted—slowly at first, like the sun peeking through a dirty window.

Giggles and eye rolls. Even Gloria's baby-faced scowl faded. And that was the thing—Vivian didn't need everyone happy. She just needed them laughing, even if it was at her expense.

If she managed that, they weren't thinking about leaving. They weren't hurting, and she couldn't have those she loved in pain. She kept up the game until, at last, Annie cracked a smile. Taryn didn't, but she didn't grumble either. That was progress.

That afternoon, she corralled Isabel and Gloria behind the linen cupboard as though she was planning a jailbreak. "Mission: Sacred Jelly Bean Ritual," she whispered. "We sneak into the littles' dormitory. Two beans in every shoe. Tell the littles it's a holy tradition for good luck. Trust me—they'll eat it up."

"Aye, you're bricky," Isabel said, her gray eyes sparkling.

Vivian wiggled her eyebrows. "You say that like it's new information."

Gloria grinned. Isabel sighed. That was a yes from both.

The three of them tiptoed through the corridors that night like spies, stifling laughter as Vivian muttered "Blessed Be the Beans" with every sugar-drop offering.

By morning, the younger girls were squealing, hopping around in stockings and shouting about miracles and candy blessings.

Vivian played innocent, of course. Who, her? Shenanigans? Never.

But the atmosphere lightened. Maybe not safe. Not with placements looming and Sister Catherine always finding fault with one of them. But perhaps, she could hold the seven of them together, just a little longer. They were her crew, these girls.

And until they pried her from the Rose's front gates, she'd keep 'em laughing to not have to face the truth—that the only real home she'd ever had was breaking apart.

Vivian knew the fun wouldn't last. It never did— not under Sister Catherine's hawk-eyed reign.

The younger girls were still chattering about the "blessed jelly bean tradition" when the storm hit just after breakfast. It wasn't thunder, but worse.

Sister Catherine.

She swept into the dining room like a winter wind with no mercy—her eyes narrowed and her mouth already twisted into what Vivian privately called the "Pursed Lips of Doom."

"Who," the nun snapped, "put candy in the wee ones' shoes?"

Dead silence. Even the littlest girls froze, mid-giggle.

Vivian stepped forward before anyone else could blink. "That'd be me," she said, crossing her arms like a barricade. "Captain of the Holy Jelly Bean Order."

Sister Catherine's nostrils flared. "You think this is a joke?"

Vivian shrugged. "That's sort of the point, isn't it?"

The woman's tone dropped dangerously low.

"You encourage irreverence. Chaos. Disobedience."

"And a wee bit of gigglemugging," Vivian shot back. "We can't forget that one."

Gasps from the girls punctuated her rebellion. It wasn't cheeky anymore—this was full-on mutiny, but Vivian stood her ground like a boulder with copper curls and a stubborn streak a mile wide.

"You will not cause unruliness," Sister Catherine hissed.

"I'm helping them survive and find joy when they can, because most of them don't remember what that feels like."

Sister Catherine's mouth opened, but Vivian didn't let her speak.

"You want discipline, fine. I'll scrub every floor from here to Dublin, but don't make them feel bad for enjoying a little fun."

The tension followed until Sister Catherine snapped, "My office. Now."

Vivian grinned—not because she wasn't scared, but because fear only had power if you let it show. As she marched down the corridor toward another lecture, another punishment, Vivian didn't look back. She knew the girls were still watching her—wide-eyed, half in awe, and half in horror. Let them see her take the fire—and know someone would.

~ ~ ~

A few hours later, Vivian sat on the cold bench outside Sister Catherine's office, knuckles red from scrubbing. After the first tongue lashing and hours of penitent chores, she'd get a follow up scolding before it was done. When you mouth off to a nun, you get the full works— floors, laundry, and silence. Not a word while she worked—just the sharp bark of commands and the judgmental echo of boots on tile.

Sister Catherine hadn't even raised her voice during the scolding. She didn't need to, for her words were knives. "You are not clever, Miss Dunne. You are reckless. You are not protecting them. You are encouraging weakness."

Vivian had bitten the inside of her cheek so hard she tasted blood. Not because it hurt—she'd had worse—but because she wouldn't let Catherine see her flinch.

After Sister Catherine finally shooed her from her presence, she sat alone on the bench, scrub bucket beside her, and her shoes soaked through. Then came the patter of little feet.

Vivian didn't look up at first. She knew that step. It was the littlest of the littles. Six years old. Tiny enough to vanish behind a laundry line. Brave enough to sneak past the dormitory curfew if she thought you needed her.

"Did you get in trouble?" The wee one asked, barely above a whisper.

Vivian didn't answer. Just leaned back against the stone wall, arms behind her head as though she couldn't be bothered.

The tiny girl came closer. She was clutching something—her handful of candy.
Vivian frowned. "What are you doing here?"

The little one held out her hand as solemn as anything. "I saved the jelly beans. The girls told me to eat the candy, but I didn't want to forget how special this day was and how happy you made us."

Vivian stared at her for a second. That stupid lump—tight and hot—rose in her throat before she could stop it. "You're supposed to eat candy, not hoard it."

The child blinked at her. "But if I eat it, I won't remember the day when everyone laughed."

Vivian looked away fast and swallowed hard. "Then I guess we'll just have to prank you again next week, huh? For memory's sake."

The small girl nodded, closed her fist around her treasure, and reached up—quick as anything—to wrap her skinny arms around Vivian. "Thank you, Captain."

And just like that, battle-hardened and fire-forged, Vivian went still. She didn't hug back—not with arms—but she didn't stop her either. She'd let the wee lassie hang on.

Maybe her strong defenses wouldn't last. Maybe she'd never make a real difference or be sent anywhere but kitchens or nurseries or places that didn't want her loud laugh and sharper tongue. But for now? She was somebody's captain.

That evening, Vivian headed to the attic hunting for a stash of contraband licorice and hoping to escape Sister Catherine's cruel words still echoing in her skull—when her fingers brushed the edge of something dusty and wooden. A small chest with no lock or label, her curiosity peaked stronger than caution.

She opened the lid.

Inside were letters. Dozens of yellowed papers with crumbling corners and faded ink. At the very top, an announcement in simple script read, For those who come after us. Don't forget we were here too.

Vivian's heart clenched. She solemnly carried the box back to the large open dormitory where the seven of them lived in close quarters. Sometimes too close. She set the box on the frayed rug as though it was holy.

"Come and see the treasure trove of letters I found!"

And one by one, the girls gathered—perhaps because of the reverent way she touched it. Isabel was first to kneel, reaching for a letter as if afraid it might vanish. Gloria sat close behind her, golden pigtails flopping over her arms.

Fiona hovered next to Annie, while Taryn set down her mending.

Cassie was the first to read her chosen missive. She pushed her round spectacles up on her nose. "'I'm leaving tomorrow. They told me I'll be a kitchen maid in a place I can't pronounce. I'm pretending I'm brave, but I'm scared everyone will forget I was ever here.—

Martha, 1866'"

Fiona was almost inaudible. "Goodness, she could've been me." She read the letter she'd chosen. "'I never told anyone, but I used to stay awake for hours and listen while the others slept, just to hear the other girls breathing. That's what home sounds like.—Josephine, 1867'"

Gloria sniffled back tears. "Me too."

"Nae. Don't cry, Gloria." Isabel interrupted, her dark eyes pleading. She didn't want this to descend into blubbering. She flipped her black braid and read her chosen letter, hoping it'd be happier. "'They say I'll have my own room, but what's the point if no one there knows me? I don't want a family who only wants a servant.—Lillian, 1870'"

The room was silent but thick with things none of them had said aloud. The fear of leaving, of being forgotten, of being a name on some paper no one would ever read again.

Vivian looked around at them—her sisters. She straightened her spine and forced her grin—the one with both dimples showing.

"All right, lassies," she said, almost teasing. "Meltdown's over. Enough of the ghost letters."

Gloria shot her a glare. "You're the one who brought them out."

"Yes, well. That was before we turned into puddles." Vivian stood, brushing off her skirt. "Listen. It's okay to feel stuff. Sure. But we don't need to get the morbs."

Isabel scowled. "Nae, but we deserve to know the

truth."

Vivian shook her head. "The truth is—we're still here and together. So, until the day we get shipped off, we laugh, eat terrible stew, play stupid games, and stick together. Deal?"

Gloria's hand shot up as though they were in school. "Can we enjoy a few more shenanigans with the younger littles before you go?"

Vivian barked a laugh. "Only if you want a legacy worth remembering."

Gloria cracked a smile, and Fiona nodded. Even Isabel sighed and gave the smallest of smirks.

Vivian lifted the open box, the letters now scattered like petals on the rug. The girls picked them up and placed them in the chest as each one whispered, "We won't forget you."

Long after her roommates had fallen asleep, Vivian wrote her own letter to add to the box.

Dear Whoever Finds This,

If you're reading this, I guess you're like me. Waiting and pretending you're not scared to leave the only home you've ever known, even if it's got leaky windows and rules like fences. They call us orphans as though that explains everything. But I'm more than that. We all are.

People call me Captain. Mostly because I talk loud and act as though I'm in charge, but the truth is—I just don't want anyone else to feel as alone as I did when I got here.

I was nine, and I'd already been through four places. One house burned down. I was locked out of another. People forgot me fast, but not here. At Irish Rose, they saw me, but now it's all ending again.

I pretend it doesn't hurt. Tonight, we read letters from the ones who left before us. They were scared too. But you know what I saw in those letters? Those girls mattered, and they still matter.

So, if you're scared—good. It means you care. Be brave. Be louder than the fear. Be someone the little ones look up to, even if you don't think you deserve it. And when you leave, don't forget who you became by being here. Even if they never say my name again, I was here.

—Vivian Dunne, Captain of the Irish Rose, 1876.

CHAPTER 4

The next morning, Fiona Donnelly lit the chapel stove an hour before prayers, long before the other girls stirred. The small cast-iron box crackled to life, spitting embers and shadows along the stone floor. She stood close, letting the warmth bleed into her palms as she rubbed her hands together.

It was always peaceful before dawn, and that was how she liked it.

As the oldest, by the time the younger girls fumbled with stockings and braids, she would have readied the chapel, steeped the tea, and stoked the kitchen hearth. No one asked her to do these things. She just did it because someone had to, and that someone had always been her. Moreover, she was the assistant cook, the keeper of all things domestic.

The others called her "Matriarch," a name she resented, not because it wasn't true, but because it reminded her that she'd likely never be a mother, only a servant. The name was a cruel echo of what she had lost, her precious mama, a title that mocked the ache of a childhood she could never reclaim. And yet, she had chosen this role—protector, caretaker, culinarian—for every younger girl who needed her. It was the only way she knew how to heal—by being what she had once needed most.

She walked to the Advent wreath at the front of the chapel and checked the candles. The first, hope, had burned two nights ago. She touched the cold, hard wax. She'd been the one to light it. She hadn't wanted to do so, yet Sister Rose had caught her lingering near the altar and smiled that knowing smile. "You're the eldest," she'd said, as though it was a blessing instead of a burden. "The first must be yours."

So Fiona had lit the candle with trembling hands and whispered a prayer she wasn't sure she believed in. "Aye, Lord. Please don't let me shatter when we all leave. When we're separated and flung to the four corners of who knows where."

She had never told anyone—not even Cassie or Isabel—that she sometimes woke in the night, gripped by the fear that she'd built her whole identity on being the perfect mother figure and holding everyone else together. As her mother had tried, and failed, to do.

When she left, and when the girls she'd embraced as sisters in her own broken way scattered to homes that didn't know them, she'd crumble into dust. After all, who was Fiona Donnelly without someone to take care of? She'd be hidden in the kitchens without her friends. Without the only sisters she'd ever known.

And underneath that fear was a seething anger toward a world that was unfair. A world that accused people and destroyed families and …

By the time she headed to the kitchen to continue her duties, the kitchen already buzzed with the familiar rhythm of breakfast, Sister Bernadette overseeing the preparations while Vivian barked orders with her usual cheer. Gloria hummed, clinging to Isabel's side as the two poured tumblers of milk. Cassie corrected Gloria's grammar, and Annie and Taryn actually speaking while setting the table.

Fiona stood at the edge of it all, arms folded, watching. A part of the group—but not.

Sister Rose entered just as the tea was poured. "Looks as though things are in order. Fiona, may I have a word?"

Her stomach flipped. "Aye, Sister."

They stepped into the corridor where the smell of cooking oats and woodsmoke faded. "I've had a request," Sister Rose smoothed her veil. "The Little Sisters of St. Joseph in Syracuse need help and their cook just retired. With your culinary skills, you'd serve as the head cook. It would be a great start to a possible career." Syracuse? So far away?

Fiona sucked in a steadying breath. "When?"

Sister Rose paused. "After Epiphany. January seventh. You'd be the first to leave."
The words landed like a stone. So soon.

"I understand." What else was there to say? She was the eldest. She was expected to go first, but the thought made her ill. The Irish Rose was the only safe place she'd known. Ever.

"You don't have to be strong all the time, Fiona." Sister Rose touched her shoulder.
Fiona blinked.

"You're a gifted cook, my daughter, and you have a bright future ahead of you. I know what you've done for these girls. The way you've cared for and protected them."

"But the wee tykes aren't mine. No one is." "No," Sister Rose agreed. "But you made them feel as though they belonged, safe and loved. And you have a special touch for cooking their meals and serving them as if you're offering them a feast instead of the meager fare they get. That is no small thing."

Fiona nodded, her throat tight. "Thank you, Sister. May I be excused?"

Sister Rose patted her arm. "Of course."

She returned to the kitchen as if nothing had changed. But everything had changed, and still, she had to feed the girls.

So she did.

By midmorning, the kitchen was clean, the soup simmered on the back burner, and she had a few moments to herself.

She fled to the attic. It was her hiding place—beside the crates of old linens and worn hymnals, up where the eaves creaked and the pigeons nested. The others thought she came up here to be alone. What they didn't know was that she came here to cry.

She sat on the old trunk and let the tears come—controlled at first, then ragged. She buried her face in her hands.

Fiona thought of Isabel, who still looked at her as though she held the answers. Of Gloria, who tucked herself into Fiona's arms during storms. Of Cassie's admiration, Vivian's blustering affection, and Taryn's rare but honest thanks. And Annie— wounded, quiet

Annie—who had once whispered to her, "You're the only one who knows how to make things feel safe."

Who would they run to when she was gone? Who would she be? This new post as cook at The Little Sisters of St. Joseph could never give her a treasured group of friends like her Irish Rose sisters.
"Fiona?"

She turned, startled that Isabel stood in the attic doorway, flushed from climbing the steep stairs.

Fiona blinked, brushing at the tears that ran down her cheeks.

"Isabel. What are you doing up here?"

"I saw you come up here. Upset. I thought maybe…" Isabel hesitated, her fingers curling around the doorframe. "Maybe you were feeling poorly and didn't want to be alone."

Fiona tried to offer a smile, but it collapsed halfway. She turned her back to the girl and stared out the attic window where the sky was the gray of coming rain. "Pay me no heed. Some things are easier alone."

"Aye, but you're not alone." Isabel stepped in. "Not unless you want to be."

Fiona swallowed hard. "They all think I'm so steady, and so sure of what comes next. Ach…they don't know the whole of me."

"But I do." Isabel didn't waver. "I remember what you told me about your mum and what they said she did."

Fiona's shoulders stiffened. That memory was a bruise she kept pressing, as if pain would teach her not to forget.

The memory flooded her mind as if it happened yesterday, though it was a six-year lifetime ago. The kitchen smelled like rosemary and smoke. Fiona sat at the corner table, peeling potatoes with hands too small for the task, her eyes stinging not from the onions, but from an impending doom she didn't understand.

Her sweet mum had raised her as a child whose papa had died in the war. But she'd heard the rumors and was called a "bastard" though she hadn't known what that meant. Yet she was loved.

Her mother shuffled from stove to sink, her apron stained with flour and broth. "Hurry with those potatoes, lassie." Mama hummed as she worked—a low, soothing melody, the one she always made when she was thinking too hard.

Then a sharp knock came, one that demanded to be answered immediately.

Her mother paused, a spoon still in her hand.

"Fiona. Go to your room."

Fiona froze. Her mother never used that tone—not for her.

The knock came again, and before either of them moved, the door swung open, and two uniformed officers stepped inside as though they belonged there. One glanced around at the kitchen at the copper pots and the hand-stitched curtains on the window, and said, "Maeve King?"

"That'd be me." Mama said.

Fiona shook her head. "My mum didn't do anything wrong!"

"She's not in trouble," the older officer lied. "We just have a few questions."

But they still put cuffs on her wrists and led her out through the garden gate.

Mama didn't cry or fight them or object. She just looked back at Fiona, her dark eyes full of something fierce and tender and said, "Don't forget who you are, lass. No matter what they say."

The last officer shut the door behind them, the silence like a tomb. Fiona stood there for a long time. The potatoes sat in cold water, the bread was left to overbake, and the rosemary turned bitter in the pan.

She sat there all alone, an abandoned nine-yearold in the last place her mother's scent still lingered. But before the day was done, she was fetched by a lady officer and sent to the Irish Rose Orphan Asylum for Girls.

In the weeks following, the nuns whispered, and the newspapers printed lies. The family Mama cooked for claimed a terrible illness, pointed fingers, and sowed doubt. There was no conviction, no real evidence, but Mama stayed in jail and soon died of pneumonia.

For years afterward, no one talked about her mother and probably assumed the worst. But Fiona knew the truth—her mother had given everything to that family and to her, but the world punished her for being poor, for being kind.

And so, Fiona stopped being the girl who waited for her mother to come back—on the day she started cooking at the Irish Rose. Thankfully, the nuns never pointed a finger at her or thought she'd poison the girls. Instead, they trusted her.

"She didn't do it," Fiona voiced her pain, her words bitter. "Aye, but that didn't matter. Everyone accused her as if she had, and she died because of it."

"Aye, but she loved you," Isabel agreed. "That's what I remember most from what you told me. How she made you lavender scones when you were scared, and how she worked so hard, even when people whispered behind her back." She paused before continuing. "I think it's time to let go of the shame and pay it no heed. You didn't do anything wrong, and neither did she."

The attic fell silent but for the creak of the floorboards beneath Fiona's feet as she crossed to Isabel and pulled her into a fierce, sudden hug.

"Aye, I don't want to run from it anymore. I want to take all that pain and use it for good. I want to be the kind of cook my mother would have been proud of, not because of where I came from, but because I will choose who I become."

Isabel's arms tightened around her. "Then you will."

Fiona drew back, nodding. She swiped at a few tears, steeling her resolve. "I'll make the crackin' best food anyone has ever tasted. Aye, I'll make them feel safe and full and at home, even if I never find mine again."

Somewhere downstairs, a younger girl cried out in fear. Fiona and Isabel both turned toward the cry, instinctive protectiveness rising.

"Aye, I'll go and get her." Isabel headed toward the stairs.

"Nae." Fiona held up a hand. "I've got her." And as she descended into the dim light of the hall, a tad bit more confidence emerged.

Maybe the past wouldn't own her anymore, after all.

CHAPTER 5

Isabel Sweeney walked the halls of the Irish Rose Orphan Asylum with grace, each step measured, her spine held straight the way her mother used to. Not stiff—never that—but steady, elegant, the kind of posture that drew refinement around her like a protective shawl.

The other girls noticed, of course. She sensed their gazes even when they pretended not to look, their chatter dying as she passed. "You seem older than fourteen, Izzy," they'd murmur. "More like a teacher…or a nun."

She never corrected them. Let them wonder. Let them think she was something more, for she had to be— at least for her sister.

She had watched her mother move with such grace and elegance, like a ballerina, before the coughing started, before her hands trembled too much to finish the fine embroidery that brought in just enough for tea and rent. Isabel had memorized the way Mama's chin lifted, how her perfection and stillness could command a room.

She mimicked it then—and now—because it kept her mother close, and it gave her something solid to stand on when everything else had fallen apart.

Isabel watched everything through veiled glances, like a bird hidden in the trees. She noticed how Sister Catherine's clipped reprimands echoed down the corridor, and how the bickering of restless girls after supper often brought tears or anger.

The girls all looked to her to be unwavering, unaffected— as if she were a fixed point in a shifting world. She wasn't a leader. No. But her steadiness somehow made them feel safe, as if the world wouldn't fall apart unless she crumbled. So, she wouldn't. Ever.

The girls called her Izzy, especially her baby sister, Gloria. Just a year apart, they had always been a pair. The other girls teased, and called them the Irish Twins, but Isabel didn't mind. For the Irish, being an Irish Twin was a badge of honor somehow, though she was a full thirteen months older. But they were inseparable, and Gloria had needed her from the day she was born—even more from the moment they walked through the gates of the asylum six years ago.

Isabel still remembered that day—the gray sky overhead, the tiny fragility of her little sister's hand in hers, how tightly she had gripped it, refusing to let go. She still didn't let go.

Gloria was so unlike her—hesitant, clinging to things Isabel had long ago buried. But they belonged to each other, and that hadn't changed, not since Mama's fingers grew too unsteady for stitching and Papa stopped coming home after his tragic accident at the docks.

During those first days of writing lessons at Irish Rose, Sister Catherine, the formidable head teacher, had noticed Isabel's neat penmanship, her assignments written in tidy script with artistic curled capital letters.

Her mother had taught her well, and Isabel had taken great care to be perfect with every curve of ink. She made every stroke exact, her letters looped just enough to look proper and elegant and beautiful like something from an heirloom Bible or a fine law book, or from one of the ledgers her father used to keep. Sister Catherine hadn't said anything then—she just watched, her eyes sharp and discerning behind her wire-rimmed spectacles.

But a year later, when the regular secretary's health faltered, Sister Rose called Isabel to her study. "Child, in the afternoons, you'll learn here." She offered her a seat at the broad, ink-stained desk. "But only if you are willing to do the work with great care. Attention to detail is not a small thing in the sight of the Almighty."

Isabel had nodded, already reaching for the pen. Of course, she was willing. Care was the one thing she had to give.

And Isabel was careful. Every line, every letter, was a thread she could control in a world that often unraveled without warning. She soon became Sister Rose's secretary-in-training—sorting ledgers, copying correspondence, organizing rosters, and more and more, taking dictation in her own confident hand. When left alone with the ink and parchment, she let her secret artistry slip in with little flourishes or elegant capitals.

Letters that looked as though they were carved in glass. She dreamed, sometimes, of becoming a calligrapher. An artist. But that wasn't a life for orphan girls. That kind of elegant purpose was for the daughters of shipping magnates and foreign dignitaries—the girls who sat in the front pews on visiting days, whose lives were etched in golden ink.

Late one evening, after lights-out, Isabel found herself still seated at the desk in the candlelit office, shoulders tense, hands ink-smeared. She had miscopied a name. Something small, but it had set off a tightness in her chest that she couldn't shake. Sister Rose came in, her presence somehow known before she spoke.

"You fear making mistakes too much, Isabel." She came to stand behind her and patted her shoulder. "Perfection is a hard god to serve."

Isabel didn't answer at first. She blinked down at the parchment, the candlelight dancing across her carefully penned lines. When she spoke, her voice cracked. "Aye, but I'm afraid…that if I stop being good at all of this, there won't be anything left of me to give."

Sister Rose didn't scold. She rested a hand on Isabel's shoulder. "Oh child, there is so much more to you than ink and obedience. You must learn that God doesn't expect perfection. He just wants the whole of you."

That night, they talked—about God and fear and talent and calling. Isabel didn't have all the answers by the time she returned to her bunk, but she had something else. A reticent courage. A sense that maybe her gift meant something, even if the world didn't know where to put it yet.

And in that silence, with her sister's steady breathing next to her, Isabel made herself a vow. She would use her gifts, even if just for letters and ledgers. She would learn and grow and keep her hand steady, because someday there might be a place where a girl like her was needed not for what she had survived, but for what she could create.

Yet she still struggled and knew how to disappear. She didn't vanish, exactly—just hid herself, tucked her words away like folded linens, and smiled at the right moments. The trick was to listen, and Isabel had always been a listener.

It's how she survived her first days at Irish Rose, the one child in the dormitory with a Spanish name and an Irish accent, and clothes two sizes too large. While the other girls sparred and sulked, she observed from behind a curtain of long black hair.

Eventually, she learned the rhythm of the place— the way Sister Agnes hummed when she was worried, how Fiona pressed her lips together when she was about to take charge, and how her sister wavered when she felt afraid.

Gloria, her timid Little Lark, with her round baby face and light green eyes, fared worse than herself. As the youngest of the older girls, she tried to be brave but often failed.

Even all these years later, Isabel's hand still ached from how Gloria clutched it during prayers last night. Isabel hadn't said anything. She just let Gloria hold her hand, because Gloria always held on, and Isabel had never once made her let go.

But this Advent, everything was changing. She could feel it in her anxious sister, clinging to her and more often than not, succumbing to tears.

That afternoon, Isabel found Gloria in the laundry room, sitting at the sorting table with her head in her hands. The steam from the hot irons made the air thick and damp, and the windows wept with condensation.

Isabel slipped onto the wooden stool next to her sister. "Blathers, lass. I thought you were with Cassie."

Gloria shook her head, her light brown braids flapping against her shoulders. "She's busy writing, so she didn't notice when I left."

Isabel didn't ask more, for there was nothing that would help. Her sweet sister never felt safe around anyone but her, so she took Gloria's hand and let the unity settle between them.

After a moment, Gloria whispered, "They're going to separate us, aren't they?"

The question wasn't new. Gloria asked it at least once a week. But this time, something had changed—

less panic and more resignation, as if she'd already accepted the answer.

Isabel squeezed her hand. "We don't know that."

Gloria looked up, her luminous green eyes teary, her face blotchy. "You always say that, but you don't believe it."

Isabel hesitated. "Nae, I don't."

Gloria let out a small, wounded whimper and dropped her head again. A few big, fat tears spilled onto the table.

"Aye, lass. I'm sorry," Isabel rubbed a hand over her sister's golden hair. Lying wouldn't help either of them anymore.

"Will you forget me?" Gloria asked just above a whisper.

Isabel moved her free hand to Gloria's back, rubbing warm circles. "Nae. Never! You're my precious little sister, my Little Lark, and my family."

"I bet you'll be so busy that you'll not have time to remember me," Gloria murmured. "Some family will want you to teach their children or transcribe letters or—

who knows what. Maybe even be a famous calligrapher or artist. You're clever and gifted. I'm just…" Her voice cracked. "I'm just a mouth to feed."

Something splintered inside Isabel. She turned so they were face to face. "Nae! You are not just a mouth to feed. You are compassionate, kind, elegant, and wellmannered. The perfect lady's maid—or maybe even a famous singer one day. Who knows? You are talented enough. Besides, you make me laugh even when I want to cry. You remember everyone's birthdays and sing in your sleep."

Gloria's brows lifted. "I do?"

Isabel smiled. "Terribly. But yes."

Gloria gave a small laugh that turned into a sob. Isabel caught her as she sagged forward, and they held each other for a long time until her shoulder was damp from tears.

"I don't want to leave you," Gloria whispered.

Isabel frowned. "Aye. I don't want to leave you either."

That evening, after supper, Isabel climbed to the attic where she joined Fiona, her closest friend besides her sister. Fiona already sat there, arms wrapped around herself. She looked older up here. More like twenty than sixteen.

"I brought you some tea." Isabel offered her the cup.

Fiona turned. "'Tis kind of you, but you didn't have to."

"I wanted to."

Fiona nodded, accepting it with an, "Aye. Thank you." She sounded less brittle than earlier.

They sat in silence, but Isabel didn't mind. Both of them seemed lost in thoughts of the future.

After a while, Fiona spoke. "Do you think we'll lose each other for good and never have the chance to reconnect? That would be a rotten bit of luck, if you ask me."

Isabel considered the question, then answered with the certainty she kept tucked beneath her gentle exterior. "Nae, but I think we'll have to work hard to keep each other close. We can write letters, share stories, and stay connected. I think the work will be worth it."

Fiona turned her head. Their eyes met. "Aye, my friend. You're wiser than most adults I know."

Isabel shrugged. "Nae, I just listen a lot, and keep my mouth shut."

Fiona gave a faint huff of amusement. "Well, keep on jabbering. I might need you to remind me who I am once I get to Syracuse."

Isabel's chest tightened. So, it was true— Fiona would be the first to go.

"Aye, I will." She swallowed the lump in her throat. "I promise."

As Isabel lay in bed that night, Gloria curled beside her like always, she stared up at the ceiling and whispered a prayer. A week ago, Gloria had squished their narrow beds together as they had when they first came to the orphanage. She wanted to be as close as she could for as long as she could—before they were forever separated.

In truth, so did Isabel. She whispered in the dark, "Lord, if You're really here…help all of us with the changes to come."

She didn't ask for a miracle.

She just asked for the threads between them to hold.

CHAPTER 6

Gloria Sweeney kept her hands submerged in the cold rinse water, washing a fine chemise in practiced circles. Around her, the slap of wet linens and the clatter of a bucket reminded her others still had chores to finish too.

Outside, the sky was a pale dove gray that made her feel as though the day never quite woke up.

She hummed as her fingers moved over the fabric, gentle but firm—as Sister Agnes had taught her. "Even silk can survive scrubbing, if the hands are gentle," she'd said.

For the past few years under her tutelage, Gloria had tried to have the right skills to one day be a fine lady's maid. She'd learned how to sew, care for clothing, style hair, and clean fine jewelry, though much of the instruction lacked true experience given the sister had taken a vow of poverty. She tried to be good enough, careful enough, and reserved enough, but would that matter when the sisters sent her away—or sent Isabel away—and separated them?

She wrung out the chemise and draped it over the line, stepping back on her heels. The back of her damp skirt clung to her knees. She brushed her long hair aside. Thank goodness. Finished for the day.

What happened to a girl who was almost ready to be a lady's maid but not quite? Would she be sent away to become a common housemaid? A scullery girl scrubbing floors in a place where no one even noticed the skills she'd learned? The thought made her chest ache.

Just then, the orphanage cat, Mouser, let out a long, loud yowl. Gloria pulled a crust of bread from her pocket, taking it to Mouser, who was curled up on the windowsill across the room. The old jet-black tomcat opened one green eye, flicked his ear, and resumed grooming the fur between his toes as if she were just another passing shadow.

Gloria knelt beside the animal. "Aye, Sister Agnes says bread's no good for cats, but you don't seem to mind."

Mouser didn't answer, of course, but he rose with a stretch and ambled to greet her, his tail curling like a ribbon. Gloria smiled and broke the crust into smaller pieces, laying them on the nearby step. The cat rubbed against her knees before sitting down to eat, dignified and graceful.

"I think you're the only one in this place who likes me without question, beside my sister," she whispered, brushing his side. "Not because I'm helpful or quiet or good at starching collars. Just because I'm me."

The cat gave a low, approving purr. "I'm glad you chose me."

And he had. Out of all the girls, Mouser had followed her the first time she left warm milk in the sewing room. He found her during laundry duty, sat beside her during garden prayers, slept in her basket of folded linens once during a thunderstorm—and after that, she had secretly hoped he'd sleep there every time.

But he wouldn't be coming with her if a post for service opened. Isabel's probable position was already being whispered about, and they might come looking for Gloria next, no matter what Izzy said. Not as a lady's maid yet, for she was too young, Sister Agnes had said, but they'd send her out to do some other kind of work. A housemaid. A scullery girl. A laundress. And they wouldn't take a cat, not even one with expressive ears and a loving gaze.

"I don't know how to do anything without you and Isabel," she murmured, running a hand down Mouser's back. "You know when I'm scared before I do. You always come when I've had a hard day. Like yesterday, when Sister Catherine said I was too timid to ever be noticed by a proper lady."

Mouser finished the last of the crust and jumped up beside her, pressing his forehead against her arm. Gloria turned at her sister's familiar footfalls.

"Aye, I knew I'd find you here." Isabel's dark skirt swished as she stepped into the room. She looked older than fourteen in the late-afternoon light— straighter, more certain—her dark eyes and darker hair giving her a dignified appearance.

Gloria always felt like a fragile lamp wick beside her sister—small and flickering, though she tried to give off a steady glow.

"You missed lunch." Isabel motioned for her to sit so she could braid Gloria's hair for chapel. "Sister Catherine saved you bread and broth."

Gloria shrugged and plunked down on the stool. "Aye. I wasn't hungry and still had several items to wash."

Isabel gave her a look. "Nae, sis. You're always hungry after lessons."

"I just didn't feel like eating." Gloria bit her lip.

Isabel was quiet for a moment as she began braiding. "You're feeling poorly about the notice, right? The one on Sister Agnes's desk."

Gloria wrung her hands. "Blathers. They've found you a placement into service, and you're leaving me."

Isabel sighed. "Aye, they think it's time. I heard Sister Agnes say, 'she's smart enough to help with books in a shop or in an office somewhere.' But I'll make sure it won't be far from you."

Gloria let out a great sigh. "And either I'll be sent away or left here without all of you? How will I survive all alone?"

Isabel sighed. "You're still thirteen, so you're not likely to be going anywhere yet, and you'll be safe here without me."

A small moan escaped unbidden. "But what if they say I have to leave and send me away? They can't keep me here forever."

"You're the youngest of us, my Little Lark." Isabel said. "And if they send you someplace bad, I'll come for you, wherever you're sent."

Gloria swallowed. "What if I'm not good enough to be a lady's maid? What if they put me in a kitchen, or—what if no one even notices I'm trying?" "Aye. You think no one notices you?" Isabel's eyes flashed. "Gloria, the sisters say you've excelled at your lessons, and you calm a room just by standing in it. And you sing like a lark. That's not nothing."

"But I'm not like you. I don't have clever answers. I don't speak up—"

"Because you listen," Isabel cut in. "You notice things and remember how people take their tea. You know how to soothe a child's crying without saying a word. You have a caring heart none of us possess. Aye. 'Tis true, you're not like me—you're better." Gloria stared at her, stunned.

"You'll make a finer lady's maid than I ever could." Isabel placed her hands on her shoulders. "Even Sister Agnes knows it. She says you are 'grace wrapped in silence.' That's her phrase, not mine."

Gloria whooshed out a gasp. "Then why does it still feel as though I'm about to be tossed aside?"

"Because you love so deeply." Isabel squeezed her hand. "And time hasn't proved to you that your compassion and concern are the very things that keep you dear in people's hearts."

She looked down at their joined hands—hers still damp and red from scrubbing, and Isabel's callused from her afternoon of mending. "When you go, promise you won't forget me."

Isabel smiled, warm and comforting. "Nae. I couldn't forget you. You're my Little Lark. My sister. My blood. Who else would remind me not to sing too loud in church?"

She managed a laugh, thin but true. The fear hadn't left entirely, but it had loosened its grip.

Isabel finished braiding her hair and gave her shoulders a gentle pat.

Gloria swallowed. "Maybe I am too timid, and perhaps that's the problem with me."

Isabel interrupted. "Blathers! Stop that. I disagree."

"Aye, I'm not ready, Izzy." Her voice caught. "I'm not ready to go where no one knows me. Where no one has green eyes, and purrs, and waits for me by the stairs. Some awful place where you aren't there."

In the distance, the chapel bell rang out, but she didn't move, Mouser curled in her lap.

"They may say he's just a cat," Isabel said, giving it a pat. "But I know what he is to you."

Gloria buried her face in the warm fur.

Isabel stroked one of her sister's pigtails. "Aye. He's your home, and so am I."

When the bell rang a second time, Mouser flicked his tail once and leapt down. He padded a few steps away, then paused and looked back, as if to say, "Go on, Little Lark. I'll be waiting here, same as always."

Gloria brushed off her skirt as she stood. The ache in her chest hadn't gone, but it had diminished a little. Mouser didn't need her to speak or smile or serve. He just needed her to be, and maybe, wherever she was placed, she could carry that kind of love with her even if she had to leave the cat behind.

Isabel tugged her forward. "We'd better get to the chapel before we're late, my Little Lark. I love you, sister. We'll make it through this. I promise."

Gloria tucked her hand in the crook of her sister's arm as they hurried to the chapel. As they entered, the chapel windows were fogged with breath and candle smoke, and the scent of pine boughs curled around the wooden pews. Voices rose in rehearsal from the front—some off-key, some uncertain—as the girls practiced lines for the annual Irish Rose Christmas pageant.

Gloria took a seat on the side bench, while Isabel joined the others. Before long, Mouser curled beside her feet, nestling in the folds of her cloak. He always found her, no matter where she went.

At the front, Annie and Taryn were at it again. "You wouldn't even know that if you hadn't left me for two years!" Taryn snapped, stepping too close.

"I had no choice," Annie shot back.

"Funny how you still got to go and live with a family—and come back with tennis awards to your credit."

"Oh? Or because no one else wanted you?"

"Lassies!" Cassie barked from her spot on the altar steps, holding up both hands like a frazzled peacemaker. "For heaven's sake. It a pageant practice, not a courtroom."

Sister Agnes looked ready to intervene, but Isabel beat her to it. "Aye! That's enough." Isabel stepped between the girls. "Stop being so scrappy. If you can't speak kindly, don't speak at all." Sister Catherine clapped her hands. "Stop it at once! You twins can both stay late to tidy the chapel."

That settled things for now. Annie huffed, and Taryn muttered, while Cassie sank back down, exasperated.

Gloria just watched as she bent down and stroked Mouser's fur, hiding and hoping to disappear into the woodwork.

Isabel tugged her from her seat. "Gloria. Come."

Her heart fluttered. She stood and walked to her sister's side, brushing her hair behind her ears.
Isabel smiled. "Guess what? They picked you."

Gloria blinked. "They picked me?"

"For the singing angel. Sister Agnes just told me. She said no one else sings like you and that your song stills a room."

Gloria's breath caught. "They want me to sing all by myself?" "Aye, you'll get to open the pageant," Isabel waved both arms in a wide arch. "With the first verse of 'Angels We Have Heard on High.' Alone." Gloria's hand went to her throat.

Isabel took her hand and patted it. "I know you're scared, but I've heard you sing to Mouser, and the laundry baskets, and the lilac bush when you thought no one was listening. You'll do a crackin' job of it."

Gloria swallowed. "Aye, but what if my voice shakes? What if it sounds too small?"

"It won't, and even if it does…" Isabel smiled, and it lit her whole face. "You'll still be the most beautiful angel the Irish Rose has ever seen."

A shout from the front drew their attention. Taryn had stomped off down the aisle, and Annie sat scowling near the manger.

Gloria looked from them to her sister. "I don't want to stand alone."

"You won't be," Isabel said. "I'll be there. And Mouser will sneak in and sit under your pew like always.

You'll have angels in the rafters and candlelight on your hair. Your song will be the first thing they remember."

Gloria nodded, adding a tentative shrug. "I do love to sing."

"Aye. I know."

As she returned to her seat—Mouser jumping into her lap without hesitation—Gloria felt something she hadn't felt in days.

Hope.

Maybe she could belong, after all, even without Mouser and her sister always beside her.

CHAPTER 7

The faint flicker of candlelight illuminated the dim Irish Rose chapel as it danced along the cold stone walls, casting strange, shifting figures. The air, thick with incense and the faint scent of old wood and wax, held the weight of centuries pressing in from the rafters above.

Cassie Mulberry had been assigned to lead the evening devotions—a sacred tradition that the nuns, in their wisdom, had entrusted to the older girls as they matured. It was both a responsibility and a rite of passage.

Cassie pushed her spectacles up on her nose and stood at the front of the chapel, her small frame dwarfed by the heavy lectern. Her hands, ink-stained from a long afternoon of bookkeeping, trembled as she held the well-worn page in front of her.

She read with little more than a whisper. "The Star of Bethlehem pierced the night, guiding the holy family through shadows of uncertainty. It was more than a light in the sky—it was a divine promise that even in the darkest of nights, God's hope still shines, steadfast and strong, leading all who seek hope and peace and salvation."

She paused, her gaze sweeping over the small circle of girls gathered for evening vespers. A few shifted restlessly, and one yawned. The story, which she had chosen with great care, had meaning, didn't it? The story was about more than a star. It was about direction, hope, and faith in an unseen future.

Cassie cleared her throat and folded the paper, tucking it against the cover of her journal. "I thought that maybe we could talk about what that kind of hope feels like, especially now, when we feel so lost. There's an Irish saying, 'Count your joys instead of your woes. Count your friends instead of your foes.' How about it?" The hush stretched on, broken only by the faint rustling of skirts and the creak of the pews. Even Annie, who often had something to say, just stared down at her fingers.

Cassie wasn't like the commanding Isabel or Vivian. Her words came out wrapped in logic, smoothed by study, lacking the sweetness that made people want to swallow them. And yet—she tried.

"Listen. The star didn't change any of their circumstances, and it didn't stop the cold or the danger. But it gave them something to walk toward. That's what hope does. It doesn't erase the hard things. It just…"

Vivian's voice cut through hers, low and shaky. "I don't care about some star in the sky. What matters right now is that I'm going to lose all of you."
Cassie blinked, and the other girls froze.

Vivian, always the dreamer, the one who hummed lullabies to herself in the laundry room, suddenly looked brittle. Her lip quivered, but her eyes burned cold and sad. "People leave. They get adopted, or they go off to work, and one day, we all get left behind like always. And then, there won't be any star to follow."

Cassie sighed. She felt it, too—that looming shadow of separation. The counting of days in ledgers no one else saw, and even her careful, accurate numbers couldn't solve this.

She reached across the circle, her hand outstretched but hesitant. "Viv, that's why hope matters. We might go different ways, but that doesn't mean—"

"No, Cassie." Vivian shot to her feet. "You always try to explain things away as though there's an answer in a book somewhere. But some of us are scared, and it's not going to get better just because you read a few sentences and called it meaning."

Cassie froze, her hand still hovering in midair. The hurt landed sharp and painful.

Vivian's skirts swished as she left the circle, her shoulders tense and her steps sure. The door closed too loudly behind her. The others looked to Cassie, uncertain but expecting an answer.

She swallowed hard. "We can be scared and still have hope. That's the real truth, and it doesn't have to make sense."

No one spoke, while few bowed their heads. But Cassie didn't sit back down. She just stared at the chapel's high window where the last sliver of starlight broke through the gathering dusk.

If only she truly believed her words of hope.

Cassie stayed behind after vespers as the others drifted off, their murmured goodnights trailing like puffs of wind. Her words had fallen flat again, but she didn't blame the girls. She was no Sister Rose, certain and composed, with words that drew everyone in. And she wasn't Vivian, who could charm a whole room into laughter even when she didn't mean to.

She was just Cassie Mulberry, with ink smudges on her hands and too many thoughts crammed behind her wide, furrowed brow. She opened her worn notebook, the one she'd brought from her parents' shop and used to record special moments. She turned to a precious blank page. She wrote the title in her neatest hand, underlined it twice, and began listing names.

My Seven Sisters' Talents and Hopes

Taryn. The girl with steady hands and always calm in a crisis. Serious and smart. Knows how to bandage and soothe. She wants to be a nurse.

Fiona. A culinary artist who has good instincts with food. A natural comfort-giver. Wants to be a cook.

She stared at the next name.

Vivian. The captain, so brave and imaginative. Reads to the littlest girls without being asked, and cares when someone's sad. She wants to be a schoolteacher or a nanny.

She paused there, the tip of her pencil hovering. The chapel was silent save the tick of the wall clock and the faint rustle of mice in the beams. Cassie turned the page and found it full of scribbled Latin conjugations and lines from Cicero. She erased the entire page and kept on writing.

Cassie. Precise, quick with sums, and remembers everything. Loves ledgers, neat margins, and structure. I want to be a bookkeeper. That part made sense. It was clean and safe and hers.

But what about the others? She'd have to think about those.

~ ~ ~

The next morning, during chores, Cassie caught Taryn first and asked her thoughts on what she'd written. Then Fiona, flour on her cheeks, grinned and gave her input without hesitation.

But when she approached Annie, Isabel, and Gloria at the end of midday break, the mood had changed.

Gloria had Mouser in her lap, running her fingers behind his ears, while Isabel mended a ripped hem with perfect little stitches. Annie leaned against the wall, twirling a bit of yarn in her fingers, her gaze on the frosty window.

Cassie sat beside them and opened the notebook. "I'm making a list of what we're good at and what we hope for after we leave the Irish Rose." Annie raised a brow. "What's the point of that?"

Cassie held her ground. "It's something we can hold onto. It's something real, even when everything else changes."

Gloria tilted her head. "Aye. What did you put for Vivian?"

Cassie turned the page she'd written earlier.

Isabel's eyes scanned the lines, and Gloria smiled at her own entry, Mouser still in her lap.

Cassie's gaze turned to Isabel. "What do you want, Izzy? What do you hope for?"

Isabel didn't answer right away. She closed the sewing kit and looked down at her hands. "A calligrapher, but I don't know if I get to want anything. Not when I've got Gloria to worry about or when I might be placed into a position far from here before the year ends."

Cassie's heart sank, but she didn't push her. Instead, she turned to Gloria. "You love singing, Little Lark. You light up when you do. What do you want?" "I like singing, but I expect I'll lose that, too, just like we lost Mama and our home and everything else." Gloria whispered, her arms tightening around Mouser.

Cassie looked to Annie last—the willowy one who, though a little scattered and messy at times, warmed your heart with her presence.

"I can't write mine down," Annie admitted. "Because if I do, and it doesn't happen, it'll feel worse than never having it at all."

Cassie closed the notebook. "I'll keep the page blank, until you're ready. For all of you."

They didn't respond, but Isabel leaned her shoulder against Gloria's. Annie scooted a little closer, and somewhere behind them, the chapel bell rang.

Cassie lifted a finger. "I have an idea. After everyone's asleep, let's meet in the laundry and talk some more, away from the worry of Sister Catherine appearing unawares."

Some shrugged. Others nodded. None spoke as they headed to chapel.

Could hope be taught like math? Tonight, she'd call them into a special circle of hope.

After lights-out and the corridors of the Irish Rose had fallen into their usual hush, the girls sneaked out of their beds. A few distant creaks, the soft breathing of the other sleeping girls, and the occasional snore from Sister Clare down the hall seemed as if all was at rest. But in the laundry cellar, in the cold stone and damp air, they gathered by one lit taper candle.

All seven of them.

Taryn and Fiona sat shoulder to shoulder on the overturned washtub. Vivian leaned against a shelf of lye soap and folded sheets, her arms crossed, as if she was still questioning their late-night meeting.

Gloria sat with Mouser wrapped in her shawl, eyes wide and searching. Annie stood to the side, assessing every movement, and Isabel twirled her braid with one hand, her face serious.

Cassie clutched her notebook to her chest, heart pounding harder than she ever remembered. This meeting had been her idea, and she hoped it'd be memorable. "All right, girls. This must be a pact. A real one, and not some child's game."

"Like the ones the boys do," Taryn added. "To swear loyalty before they go to war."

Vivian nodded. "Only, we are swearing to never, ever leave each other behind or forget each other."

Cassie's fingers curled tighter around the notebook. This wasn't rational, nor was it wise. If the nuns found out…. But some part of her—a part that even numbers couldn't touch—ached for something binding and permanent. Because the truth was, she couldn't bear to lose these girls either.

"We need something to mark this pact," Vivian whispered. "Like...blood." A hush fell.

Isabel grinned, but even her grin trembled. "What are we, pirates?"

"Nae." Annie shook her head. "We're sisters."

That word hit Cassie like a weight. She had never had a sister. But this group of girls was something like it. Fiona plucked a sewing needle from the pincushion on the table and sterilized it in the candle flame. No one moved.

"I'll go first," Taryn pricked the pad of her finger, and a bead of red welled up. She pressed it to a scrap of linen from the rag bin near her.

One by one, the others followed.

Vivian's hand shook, and Fiona bit her lip. Gloria flinched but held steady, and Isabel made no noise at all. Annie groaned. When it was Cassie's turn, she paused. Her hands were always ink-stained and careful.

She bit her lip and pushed the needle into her fingertip. It stung sharper than she expected, but she pressed her finger to the cloth.

Seven prints. Seven smudges. Seven girls. Seven sisters. Forever.

Cassie held the scrap in her hands, her blood mingled with theirs. Her voice shook as she spoke. "I, Cassie Mulberry, vow to always be your sister. To fight for you and remember you. To never forget who we were here, together. We are, and forever will be, The Irish Rose Sisters."

They echoed the words, each in their own way. Some with clarity, and others with choked agreement. All with tears.

Then Isabel stepped forward, pulled the cloth from Cassie's hands, and folded it reverently. "No one can ever see it, or they'll call it childish nonsense. But we will know what happened this night, and we'll always remember."

She tucked the cloth behind the loose brick near the chimney, deep in the laundry cellar's wall, hidden and eternal. Silence fell again, but this time, the cold didn't bite so hard, and the dark didn't feel so empty.

Vivian was the first to speak. "If one of us leaves, we still belong to each other, right?"

Cassie reached for her hand. "Always."

Annie linked hers next. Then Gloria. Then Isabel.

Seven girls, with fingers still tinged with blood, intertwined in the flickering candlelight. And though none of them would say it aloud, they knew that whatever came next, whether it be placements, separations, years or miles, they had sealed something deeper than fate.

They had forged a forever sisterhood, bound not just by blood, but by choice.

CHAPTER 8

It was time for their second Advent devotion as the chapel walls flickered with candlelight, and outside, snow dusted the orphanage windows like lace. Tonight, Vivian would be leading, but Sister Rose, would speak first.

The girls settled, the rustle of skirts and whispered greetings fading into a hush. Vivian sat up straight, her nerves tingling as she folded her hands in her lap. The scent of pine filled the room from the wreath on the table—a simple circle of evergreen branches cradling four candles, three purple and one rose.

"My dear girls," Sister Rose began gently, like a warm bowl of porridge with cream and sugar. Though most often found in the kitchen, she exuded wisdom from above. "Before we speak of what comes next for some of you, we want to begin with the wreath."

Vivian's gaze drifted to the flickering purple flame from the first week of Advent. The hope candle was already lit, but she would light the second one.

"This Advent wreath tradition," the sister continued, "comes from a humble pastor in Germany, a man who worked with poor children in Hamburg. To help them mark the days until Christmas, he created a great wooden wheel with little red candles for each weekday and four big white candles for the Sundays of Advent. Each candle lit signified a step closer to the birth of Christ."

Vivian listened, still and attentive. A hush settled deeper in the room, like snow falling on rooftops.

"In time," Sister Rose said, "the church adapted the wreath. Now we light three purple candles—for hope, peace, and love—and one rose- colored, for joy. Each week, we'll light a new candle."

She paused, her gaze sweeping over them. "The fifth candle, a white one to be placed in the center, we light on Christmas Eve. It is Christ's candle—His everlasting light. The circle itself reminds us that God's love has no beginning and no end. And the evergreen? That's life that endures the cold, dark winter."

Vivian swallowed. How many times had she counted the weeks until Christmas with aching joy? Now, she counted down to something else—the day she would leave all she knew to journey into the unknown.

Sister Rose paused. "So let us remember, in all seasons—especially in waiting seasons like Advent—that there is light, there is hope, there is peace and joy, and there is also love without end. Tonight, Vivian will light the candle of peace." She waved a hand for Vivian to proceed and took a seat with the other nuns.

Vivian closed her eyes for a moment. She wasn't sure she felt any peace, but she wanted to. She stood, cleared her throat, and adjusted the sheet of paper in her hands, her heart pounding. Some captain and leader of the pack she was, shaking in her boots. She took a deep gulp of air before beginning.

"I wasn't sure what to say, but I kept thinking about how, during the season of Advent, the world waited for Christ for so long, not knowing if peace would ever come again to their world. There were four hundred years of silence between the last time God spoke in the Old Testament and when Jesus came. That's a long time not to hear from God."

Vivian struck the match, and though her fingers shook a bit, she hoped no one noticed. She tilted it to light the peace candle, watching the wick flare to life and the purple wax begin to melt. The room, already dim and quiet with anticipation, seemed to lean into the flickering light.

"Tonight, we light this candle for peace."

The girls sat around the Advent wreath and watched her, their faces bathed in amber glow. Outside, snow dusted the trees and rooftops of Brooklyn. It was the kind of hush that usually settled the soul—but Vivian's heart remained restless.

She continued. "As we wait in this Advent season, peace can feel elusive." She paused to fold the sheet of paper. A moan escaped her lips, and with it, her guarded composure.

"I have to admit"—she kept her voice from quivering—"with all the changes to come and the thought of losing you, my sisters, I've been struggling to feel God's peace."

A rustle moved through the room, a slight shifting of posture—surprise from some, silent recognition from others.

"I pray and read and speak the words I know are true. But it's like reaching into a darkened room and finding nothing but emptiness." Her gaze drifted to the flame, flickering despite the subtle draft. "And some days...I wonder if God sees me and if He cares."

Stillness fell again, deeper this time. "But I think that peace isn't just a feeling. It's a person, and sometimes we find Him in the waiting itself."

No one spoke as the candle glowed. Several girls held their breath as Vivian took her seat. Annie glanced at Taryn, who sat with arms crossed. Cassie picked at a frayed thread on her stocking.

Fiona cleared her throat and sighed. "Aye, I've felt that same restlessness. It's like I've been praying into the void. I've been working and not shirkin' my duties and smiling like everything's fine. But inside, I feel as if I'm still waiting for God to give me the peace I seek."

Isabel brushed her glossy black hair from her face and smiled. "Aye, but isn't that what Advent is all about? It's not just about celebrating that Jesus came, but it's learning how to wait in the dark and choosing to believe that the light is coming even when we can't feel it yet."

She picked up a small votive candle from the table. "This wee candle's cold. It looks like nothing, but in a few seconds…" She took the peace candle and lit the wick, and a bright flame sprang to life as she returned the candle to its place in the wreath. "It burns warm and bright, and it changes everything around it. Just like Him."

Cassie wiped her tears with her sleeve. "Isaiah 9 says, 'The people walking in darkness have seen a great light.' That wasn't because they turned on a light but because the Light came to them. So maybe...faith isn't feeling certain. Maybe it's just choosing to believe He's still coming, even when everything feels hazy."

A hush hung in the room, thick and holy. Isabel handed the little white votive to Gloria, and one by one, the girls held it in their hands before passing it on.

No one spoke until the flame came to Vivian. "I think I've been pretending to be brave, but I'm scared. I don't want to go where no one knows me."

Isabel slid an arm around her. "Aye. You'll have us. Always."

Sister Rose cleared her throat. "My children, let us pause." She moved softly as she came close, her presence commanding without force. She gently took the votive from Isabel and set it on the table. "I'm proud of your honesty, and I know the unknown feels imminent and frightening. Your upcoming placements are scary, and that is why we're holding these special meetings with just you seven."

Her gaze moved from face to face. "But peace— true peace— is not found in knowing where you're going. It's found in knowing Who goes with you, as Vivian expressed so well."

The girls shifted in their seats as Sister Rose cast Vivian an affirming smile. "You may be scattered across cities and into the unknown, but you are not being cast out. You are being sent, and the Lord who called you here will walk every step of the journey ahead. Even into the unfamiliar, the lonely, and the far-away places." A lump rose in Vivian's throat at those words.

Sister Rose's eyes sparkled in the candlelight. "Peace is not the absence of fear. It is the presence of Christ in the middle of it all. And He is here with you now, even in these changes."

Vivian glanced toward the Advent wreath on the table. The candles of hope and peace burned bright. A few girls sniffled, but in Vivian's heart, grief gave way to a hint of peace.

"And now, my precious ones, I must relay some news." Sister Rose sighed, though her gaze was clear and unwavering. "One of you has received your service assignment. Tonight, some of you will receive yours as well. Remember, these are not just placements, but callings. After the New Year, you will start your journey, and I ask that you meet it with courage and grace."

A ripple went through the girls—panic for some and bowed heads for others. Vivian twisted her handkerchief in her lap. Isabel stared straight ahead, her jaw clenched. Cassie blinked hard, as if trying not to cry.

Sister Rose opened the first folded page. "Vivian Dunne."

Vivian's breath caught as she stood, her legs stiff. She made her way to the front where Sister Rose smiled and offered her the envelope. "You are to serve as a nanny assistant in a well-to-do household on Long Island. They have four children, and it's a strict but well-ordered home. The mistress watches everything with a keen eye, and rightly so. In time, you may earn a higher position, maybe even assisting in household matters."

She touched Vivian's shoulder. "You've a vibrant strength, child. Let it shine where others expect silence."

Vivian swallowed, nodded, and stepped back with trembling hands. Who else would hear of their fate this night?

Sister Rose unfolded the next paper. "Isabel Sweeney."

Isabel rose, composed as ever, though her fists were tight at her sides.

"You'll stay in Brooklyn," Sister Rose said, "and work at Lathrop, Smith & Oliphant. You'll serve as a scribe copying documents by hand. It's a wonderful opportunity—tedious work to some, but precision is a rare gift, and you possess it."

Isabel's brow furrowed. "Aye. Will I be trained for the work?"

"They will expect you to learn swiftly, but you're a talented and clever girl." Sister Rose offered her a small smile. "And take heed—one mistake in a company contract could cost hundreds. Yet you're skilled already, and they'll trust your hand before long."

Isabel gave a short nod and took her envelope, shuffling back to her seat.

"And now—Cassie Mulberry."

Cassie hesitated a moment before standing. She wobbled a bit, but her stride soon stabilized.

"Manhattan," Sister Rose said. "You'll assist with inventory for Henry Heath's manufacturing offices. It's a large operation where you'll likely help track hours, materials, and wages. It's a fine step toward bookkeeping, and your eye for numbers will serve you well, if you keep it sharp."

Cassie blinked. "Henry Heath?"

Sister Rose nodded. "He's a fine businessman, a Civil War veteran. He's exacting but fair, and if you work hard and well, you'll be noticed."

Cassie's mouth pressed into a line, but she accepted the letter with both hands. "Yes, Sister."

More names would follow in the days ahead. But for now, the room was quiet, except for the crackle of paper and the rustle of girls weighing futures they'd never chosen. Outside, the bell clanged, reminding them all that their lives had changed.

"These next steps may feel like endings," Sister Rose continued. "But they are beginnings. You were not made to stay rooted here forever. You are meant to grow up, even when it's hard. Embrace peace, hold fast to hope, and be strong. Each one of you is more capable than you believe.”

She paused, her gaze passing over each girl. “And, as an Irish proverb says, ‘may you never forget what is worth remembering, nor ever remember what is best forgotten.’”

Something in Vivian’s chest pulled tight. Her mother’s face flashed across her mind, wan and weary that last day they parted. She had clung to her mother’s apron hem, crying into the fabric. Now there would be no hem to cling to, no familiar arms to run to.

Vivian’s heart raced as she absorbed the weight of the evening, and she clutched the envelope to her chest. This wasn’t the end.

And somewhere, beneath the fear, something had already begun to grow. Perhaps it was hope.

CHAPTER 9

Annie didn't even remember who had started the frivolity. The sunny room rang with laughter and the thumps of bare feet on the floor, their beds mussed from the fun. Clean socks flew through the air like birds in a wild storm, landing on beds, girls, and the floor.

It felt as though the mounting tension had reached a boiling point, erupting like a volcano.

Annie clutched her side, breathless from laughter, as Vivian launched a rolled-up stocking across the room. It smacked Gloria square on the cheek, and the girls burst into a fresh wave of giggles. One moment, they'd been folding laundry, and the next, the dormitory was full of flying linens, shrieking joy, and a kind of unspoken relief, and just for a moment, they weren't orphans in training for service. They were just girls. Annie was mid-jump on her mattress when the door creaked open. The laughter died at once.

Sister Catherine stood in the doorway like a thundercloud—hands clenched at her sides and her jaw locked tight, her gaze sweeping the room with accusatory, deliberate fury. "What," she said, tone low and thick with venom, "is the meaning of this disgrace?" No one moved. No one spoke.

"You think this is a game?" she spat. "You think the families you are being sent to will tolerate this kind of behavior? You acting like wild animals? Like godless, foolish children with no self-control?"

Annie's stomach churned. The echo of her laughter now felt like a sin. She stepped off her bed, head bowed. Heat rose to her cheeks, but it wasn't from shame—it was from the injustice curling in her chest like a fist.

Sister Catherine strode into the center of the room, her volume rising. "You all will fail. Every one of you. You will disgrace those who raised you, and you will prove what the world already believes—that you are worthless. Orphans who know nothing but foolishness and failure."

The words struck like stones, and Annie couldn't even meet the gazes of the others. Tension hung heavy in the air, thick with humiliation. Some of the girls stared at the floor, their eyes shining with tears. Others stood frozen.

"If God turns His back on you," Sister Catherine said, cold as winter, "you will have only yourselves to blame. Clean up this room now, and stop your foolishness at once."

Then, with a final sweeping glare, she turned and walked out, her footsteps sharp and accusing as they faded down the hall.

The void after Sister Catherine's departure felt deafening, and no one moved at first.

Gloria sniffled, bending to retrieve a pillow from the floor. "Blathers! She hates us," she whispered.

"She despises us." Vivian kicked a balled-up sock toward the wall. "Treats us like we're less than dirt."

"Aye, she doesn't even see us," muttered Isabel, her face flushed with anger. "Just our mistakes."

Annie knelt near her bed and began gathering scattered laundry. The joy from moments ago had evaporated, but the pain that replaced it—sharp and unfair—left her chest aching. She wanted to be angry too.

"She shouldn't talk to us like that," Vivian continued, her brows furrowed. "Worthless? God turning His back on us? That's not even…"
"She's cruel. Just cruel." Taryn stomped a foot.

"No one should talk like that to anyone, let alone…" Isabel stopped herself.

The room swelled with murmured agreement, growing louder with each piece of bedding adjusted as they remade their beds. The sting of injustice united them, sharpening into a hot, collective fury.

Taryn slammed her cupboard door shut. "I don't care if she's a nun or the pope. I hate her!" The words dropped like stones, harsh and final.
Annie snapped a glare at her. "Taryn—"

"I do," Taryn growled. "She acts as if God belongs to her. As if she's His guard dog."

"She's wrong about us, but…," Annie huffed.

Taryn turned to face her. "Are you excusing her wickedness?"

"No." Annie rose, sock in hand. "Not her words, and I don't think God turns His back on us because we laugh or mess up, but He must forgive her too."

"Nae. She said we are nothing," Gloria murmured.

"She's wrong." Annie declared. "We're not nothing."

Vivian folded her arms. "You really believe He forgives people like her?"

Annie looked down at the sock in her hands, then out the window, where golden light still clung to the horizon. "I think He forgives all of us, even when we don't deserve it. Especially then."
An uneasy pause followed.

Taryn let out a bitter laugh. "Well, I don't forgive her. Not today—or ever." She snatched her coat from the hook, threw it over her shoulder, and stormed out of the room, slamming the door behind her hard enough to rattle the windows.

Annie exhaled, then turned and picked up another sock. She handed it to Isabel with a small smile. "Come. Let's clean up and not let cruel words be the only ones that matter today."

One by one, the girls followed her lead, putting the room back together, piece by piece. When the bell rang for lunch, echoing down the corridor, the girls filed out of the dormitory without a word, though Taryn hadn't come back.

Annie walked between Vivian and Cassie, her arms folded. Her stomach still ached from Sister Catherine's words, but she'd tried to leave them behind with the socks and other laundry. Still, words like that had a way of slicing her heart. At least Fiona, working in the kitchen, had been spared.

They entered the dining hall, where the long wooden tables were already set with bowls of stew and crusty bread. The scent of onions and thyme drifted through the air as a few younger girls giggled at a nearby table, while most of the older ones sat still.

Sister Rose stood at the head of the room, her face serene but serious. She lifted her hand, calling for silence. "My dear girls, I know this morning has been difficult, but we must not let anger steal our joy. Today, I have news for some of you."

Annie straightened, her heart thumping.

"Service placements have come through for three more of our young ladies."

Heads turned, and spoons paused mid-air.

The room grew still. Sister Rose's gentle gaze found Annie. "Annie Burns." Annie gasped.

"You will be assigned to the Buckingham Hotel in Manhattan, as a dresser—an assistant to a lady's maid. You'll help care for a prominent lady— or possibly several. Duties will include clothing care, hairdressing, cosmetics, shoe and jewelry maintenance, and, of course, discretion. Sister Agnes has taught you well, but you'll learn even more. And if you prove as trustworthy and capable as I think you are, you may one day become a lady's maid yourself."

The words landed like rain on parched soil.

Annie blinked, stunned. A dresser? In a Manhattan hotel? It was more than she'd hoped for and more than she'd dared to imagine.

Around her, the girls murmured in surprise and admiration.

Then Sister Rose said, "Taryn Burns." But she didn't look up.

A hush fell. Taryn's seat at the table remained empty. Annie glanced toward the door.

"Taryn, you will begin training in a Brooklyn almshouse, serving the elderly and infirm…" Sister Rose surveyed the room, her brows furrowed. "Where is your sister, Annie?"

"I don't know."

"All right. I'll speak to her later. And the rest of you, say nothing about the announcement I made of her placement, please."

The girls murmured, "Yes, Sister" almost in unison.

Sister Rose clicked her tongue. "And finally… Gloria Sweeney."

Gloria gasped beside Isabel.

"You will remain here for another year, Gloria," Sister Rose said, smiling. "You are young but talented, and we can use you right here where you're safe and can make friends with the other girls. You will assist Sister Agnes in instructing the middlers in lady's maid duties—sewing, ironing, and etiquette—and you'll also help with music and choir. You have a gift, and now, you'll begin to share it. And as you know, your sister, Isabel, will remain nearby as she works at Lathrop, Smith & Oliphant."

There was a small ripple of surprise, but Gloria's face bloomed into a grateful smile. Isabel squeezed her hand. It was a wonderful answer to Gloria's angst.

Annie looked down at her bowl, heart racing. The Buckingham Hotel as assistant lady's maid. Polished shoes and painted lips and secrets whispered in rooms upholstered in rich velvet. Was she ready for that world? What would Taryn say when she heard each of their assignments?

The lunchroom had almost emptied by the time Taryn returned. She slipped in through the side door, her hair wind-tossed, her cheeks pink with cold and fury. Her coat was wrinkled, and her guarded glare scanned the tables like a challenge, daring someone to speak.

Annie saw her first. "Taryn."

Her jaw twitched. "I needed to be alone." Sister Rose, who had stayed to clear a tray, noticed her too. She didn't scold but simply approached her. "Taryn," she said, "your service assignment has arrived." Taryn gulped in a breath, guarded.

"You've been placed in a Brooklyn almshouse. You'll tend to the elderly and the sick. Assist with cleaning, cooking, and personal care. Learn the basics of compassion and healing. It's hard work, but good work." She blinked. "You mean like a nurse?"

"A nurse-in-training." Sister Rose nodded.

She didn't respond at first. Her eyes gave her away—stormy and bewildered. She gave a small nod, then turned and sat beside Annie without a word.

The girls regrouped later in the dormitory, the day waning toward evening. The room felt strangely smaller now, more intimate. They curled into a loose circle near the hearth, some cross-legged on the rug, others perched on beds.

"So," Vivian said, poking the air with her comb like a pointer, "we've all got our marching orders."

Isabel gave a low whistle. "The Buckingham Hotel. That's downright crackin', Annie."

"I suppose." Annie smoothed the hem of her skirt. "But it's not like I'll be a lady. I'll just help someone to look like one."

"Still, it's better than scrubbing chamber pots in an almshouse," Taryn muttered from the edge of her bed.

Vivian shot her a look. "It's not a punishment, Taryn."

"It feels like it," she grumbled. "Rotting old people coughing in my face all day?"

Gloria frowned. "Ach, that's not fair."

Taryn leaned forward, face hard. "What if I get sick? What if I mess it up? What if someone dies while I'm supposed to be helping them?"

The room went still.

Fiona shrugged. "Aye, but what if you save someone's life?"

Taryn glanced over at her but didn't speak. "I don't know what I'm doing either."

Gloria huffed. "Teaching music to middlers? Me a teacher? Blathers. I thought I'd be sent out with the rest of you."

Annie nodded. "I'm scared too. What if I forget something important or speak when I'm not supposed to?"

Vivian wrung her hands. "I'm terrified I'll end up losing a child."

"We're all imagining the worst," Annie said.

"You sound like Sister Rose," Taryn muttered, but with less bite this time.

Annie offered her a small smile. "Maybe that's not such a bad thing."

Silence stretched between them—not heavy, but thoughtful. They sat with their fears and their hopes like folded garments packed for a long journey. None of them knew exactly what was coming, but they knew this—childhood had ended.

CHAPTER 10

After morning prayers, Gloria lit a half-used taper to light one of the many votive candles, shielding the fragile flame from the morning breeze slipping in through the drafty chapel window. The wax melted in strange stripes and glowed warm against the chill pressing in around her.

All the girls had been placed, and soon they'd be whisked off to service in homes or businesses across Brooklyn and beyond. All, that was, but her.

She would be staying here for one more year under Sister Agnes's watchful care. She had smiled and dipped her head when Sister Rose announced it, and her heart exhaled in relief, but the truth was, the relief mingled with some sadness. Though she hated to be left behind, she wasn't ready to leave the familiar corridors of the Irish Rose Orphan Asylum. Nor was she ready to leave Isabel or the moments of threading needles in

Sister Agnes's lavender-scented presence, or to say goodbye to the firelit hush of evening devotions.

She whispered a small prayer of thanks as she set the taper upright in the votive tray. She hadn't prayed for courage but for the strength to become a person worthy of being chosen when her time did come. She yearned to be one who was not so soon passed over.

Behind her, someone approached. "You always light a candle when you're worried, Little Lark," Isabel teased.

Gloria turned, her cheeks flushing. "Ach. I am." Gloria tucked a loose strand of hair behind her ear. "I don't know what my future holds, and you'll be gone. But, at least you'll still be close by, in Brooklyn, right?"

"Aye, my Little Lark, and I'll write," Isabel promised. "Whenever I can, I'll come to see you on your birthday or on Christmas or just because. You're never alone, sweet sister."

But the days had felt more fragile of late, like melting ice. As the other girls grew bolder and more talkative and more confident, Gloria just listened and observed. The thought of them leaving her nipped at her heart.

"You'd better go," Isabel said. "Sister Agnes is waiting for you."

She hugged her sister. "I'm glad you'll be near."

When Gloria arrived in the sewing room, the lamplight shone warm and golden. Bolts of wool and muslin lined the walls, and the faint, familiar scent of lavender clung to the air. Sister Agnes sat at her worktable, mending a hem with methodical grace, her needle dancing in and out as though it flew on wings instead of thread.
Except for her, the room was empty.

"Sit by me, Gloria," she said without looking up. "We're going to talk while we stitch today."

Gloria obeyed, adjusting her skirts before reaching for her embroidery hoop.

"I was sixteen," Sister Agnes began, her voice low and steady. "My older sister, Nora, was sent to work in Boston, while I was to serve on Madison Avenue." In her surprise, Gloria pricked her finger.

Sister Agnes had never shared her story.

"I hated the emptiness at night, the way it echoed in the marble halls. I hated the way my letters to Nora went unanswered. And I hated how much I wanted to be perfect, and how hard I worked for any simple nod or a word of praise. But none came."

Gloria's fingers trembled. That was what she feared the most—that she'd be invisible, that her goodness would never be enough, and that someone brighter, louder, bolder would always outshine her.

"You think kindness is forgettable." Sister Agnes paused her sewing. "But it stays with people, like sweet perfume or like stitches that hold a seam."

Gloria's throat tightened. "Aye. Sometimes I wish I were more like Isabel or Annie. They know who they are."

"You know what everyone calls you, but do you know why?"
Gloria shrugged.

"Little Lark is more than your sister's nickname. You watch and care when it matters most. You carry morning in your eyes, even when the day is gray. And you sing the heavens to earth."

Tears pricked at the corners of her vision, hot and sudden. "But what if that's not enough?"

Sister Agnes leaned forward, brushing a thread from Gloria's shoulder. "It's more than enough. The world needs watchers and feelers and keepers of light like you. You matter, Gloria." Sister Agnes continued to stitch, the pull of thread whispering in the moment.

Gloria stitched, too, but slower. She didn't know what to say until her needle snagged the linen. "I can't stop thinking that if I were gone, no one would pay any heed."

Sister Agnes paused, but she didn't look up. "Who told you that?"

"No one. That's just how it feels sometimes. I do what I'm told. But the loud girls—they're the ones who get remembered and chosen."

Sister Agnes smoothed the hem of the nightgown she was mending. "You think being quiet and careful makes you invisible?"

Gloria hesitated, then nodded. "I think and feel things, but I say too little."

After a long pause, Sister Agnes set down her needle and folded her hands. She looked at Gloria. "Do you know the story of Saint Melangell?"
Gloria blinked. "Nae."

"She was an Irish princess who dedicated her life to reflection and prayer. She was so gentle that even the wild hares trusted her. One day, a prince chased one of those hares into the forest. But when he found it at the princess's feet, he couldn't kill it. Her meekness showed him that gentleness was a blessing, a gift."

Gloria tilted her head, unsure where this was going.

"Melangell never spoke much," Sister Agnes said. "But she changed people without shouting. Without needing to be first or loud or clever. Her gentle presence was enough. Meekness is not weakness, dear one. When under God's control, it can be a powerful inner strength that puts others above themselves. The Lord Himself said that the meek shall inherit the earth."

Gloria shook her head. "But what if I'm meek because I'm afraid? What if I try to please people for fear they'll stop loving me?"

The question hung in the air, raw and trembling. Sister leaned forward and took Gloria's stitching from her. "Let me tell you something that took me too many years to learn. Love that must be earned isn't love, and you, my Little Lark, were born to be loved and cherished."

Sister Agnes touched her cheek. "Moreover, you are not invisible, Gloria, and you're not forgettable. You are the hush before the hymn and the silence in the snow. You steady the room when it quakes, and you don't even realize you do it."

A tear slipped down Gloria's cheek, but she didn't brush it away. "Aye, I just want to matter."

"Oh, Gloria, you do, more than you know. You've already learned so much here, and someday, you'll serve a lady. But, I suspect, you'll do so much more than dress her or press a hem. You'll hold her heart together when the world pulls it apart, for that's what true maids do. A true lady's maid tends to more than cloth and china."

Gloria suddenly felt older and wiser, though her hands still shook. "Aye, will you teach me how?" "I already am, but you will learn much more this next year, not just in the ways of a maid but in who you are as a child of God. I pray your talents blossom like a rose in springtime as you grow in your skills as a lady's maid, your musical aptitude, and in everything else you do."

Gloria swiped a fat tear from her cheek. "Thank you, Sister. I'm much obliged for your kind words."

~ ~ ~

The evening rehearsal felt extra special as the scent of pine and old wood wafted in the chapel air. A few stray snowflakes clung to the edges of the stained- glass windows, and candlelight flickered in wobbling halos above the girls in white.

The younger orphans, dressed in well-worn wings, fluttered about in excitement, their giggles echoing off the stone walls. Gloria stood at the front, her hands folded at her waist. Her breath rose in small clouds, and for a moment, the nerves returned—tight and familiar in her chest.

Then she remembered Sister Agnes's parting words: You steady the room when it shakes.

She inhaled. The first note left her lips as clear as the chapel bell. "Angels we have heard on high…"

The music lifted, flowing like water over smooth stone. Her song, delicate but strong, reached the corners of the chapel, wrapping the listeners in a warm and holy hush. Even the little ones stopped fidgeting, and their gazes locked on her.

"Gloria…in excelsis Deo…"

Her name echoed through the song, but not as herself—as a word that held the divine. And somehow, that made it easier to sing.

She didn't falter, and her pitch held. Her song stayed strong, and when she reached the final refrain, she let herself sing, not from her throat but from deep in her heart where she could still feel her mother's lullabies and her father's laughter echoing off shipyard beams.

When the last note hung in the air, the girls erupted.

"She sang like a real angel," one sighed.

"Can you teach us how to sing like that?" another piped up.

Gloria blinked, surprised. A few of the littlest girls came to her, tugging at her skirts, smiling up at her as though she was something rare and precious.

Her first instinct was to retreat, to downplay it, but this time, she didn't. Instead, she knelt among them, her heart beaming. "Of course, I can. It's all about listening to the notes and to the Spirit inside." One of the smallest, a red-cheeked girl, whispered, "Do you get scared before you sing?" "All the time," Gloria admitted, smiling. "But the trick is to sing, anyway."

She looked toward the flickering votive candles. Toward the one she had lit that morning for the girl she wanted to become, and for the first time, she didn't feel so far from her.

That night, Gloria lay beneath the worn quilt in the dormitory, her breath steady in the winter dark as sleet pattered against the windows. She stared up at the ceiling, lit faintly by moonlight.

Is this what it feels like to be enough?

She touched her throat and wondered if she could carry that certainty with her—into the sewing room and into her future lady's household, and into the hushed moments when doubt would return.

Maybe true confidence isn't about never being afraid. Maybe it is about doing what needs to be done, anyway—like singing through the silence and standing through the fear.

She imagined herself a year from now standing straight and speaking confidently, ready to serve a lady with grace and care. She imagined her eyes seeing what others missed as her delicate hands fastened buttons, comforted her mistress, or mended her clothes. She imagined being loved—not in spite of her gentleness, but because of it.

And in that moment, she chose to become that girl.

CHAPTER 11

The classroom smelled of mildew and chalk. Sleety rain slicked the windows, and gray light dappled everything inside with shades of bleakness. Fiona sat at her desk, her hands rough from kitchen work and her sleeves still damp from scrubbing pots with Sister Bernadette.

Sister Catherine entered with the usual hiss of vitriol, her ledger tucked under one arm like a judge's gavel. She scanned the girls—seven in total, though a few ever seemed to matter. To Sister Catherine, the obedient ones were invisible, and the defiant ones, unforgettable. Her gaze stopped on Fiona.

"Miss King." The words were cold and clipped. "Since you spend your mornings feeding bodies, perhaps you'd care to nourish our spirits. Lead us in the Lord's Prayer—in Latin."

Fiona rose, heat already rising in her chest. She clasped her hands in front of her, her voice steady at first.

"Pater noster, qui es in caelis, sanctificetur nomen tuum…"

She reached *caelificetur*, but the word snagged on her tongue. She faltered, just a moment— but it was enough.

"Speak up," Sister Catherine barked. "Or has all that kitchen steam melted your mind?"

A few girls shifted in their seats, a gasp echoing in the stillness, but no one dared move.

She cleared her throat, tried again. *"Adveniat regnum tuum…"*

"Wrong." Sister Catherine crossed the room. "Not only can you not recite a prayer, you mumble like a guttersnipe." She paused at Fiona's side. "Perhaps you inherited your mother's vile tongue."

Her spine stiffened. "Nae! Please don't talk about her."

Sister Catherine tilted her head. "Oh? I shouldn't mention the woman who bore you in sin? Who worked below stairs, and played the harlot?"

A few girls gasped—Isabel's hand flew to her mouth—but no one interrupted.

Fiona fisted her hands. "Stop! Don't speak about her."

"She poisoned the family that fed her, and then left you to poison the rest of us with your arrogance." "Nae! She didn't do it."

"Six people sick and a kitchen maid with no alibi? That's not innocence. That's wickedness."

"I said she didn't do it!" She protested an octave higher than usual.

The tension that followed seemed to scream. Sister Catherine took a deliberate step back and opened the drawer of her desk. Out came the strap holding cruel memories. "Hands," she said.

Fiona hesitated. Her jaw clenched, but slowly, she extended her palms. Her wrists trembled.

The first strike came hard and sudden. Crack.

She flinched but didn't cry out. Crack.

Her teeth dug into the inside of her cheek. Crack. By the fourth blow, her hands had gone numb. Sister Catherine leaned in close, her breath stale and bitter.

"You'll never be more than her shadow. You think scrubbing pots will make you good? You are marked, girl, and sooner or later, your true nature will come out."

Fiona looked up at her, her mind filled with loathing. She didn't blink or look away. "Then I'll scrub harder."

For a fraction of a second, Sister Catherine hesitated. Then she stepped back and snapped the strap against her desk. "Sit down."

Fiona returned to her seat. Her palms throbbed. Angry red welts pulsed on her hands as though they had a heartbeat. Her body shook, not from pain, but from the effort of not falling apart.

Isabel sat beside her, unmoving.

Fiona whispered without turning, "Nae. Don't say anything."

"You shouldn't have to take that," Isabel whispered back.

"Aye. I can take worse."

"But you shouldn't have to."

She didn't answer. Instead, she stared straight ahead.

Sister Catherine returned to the front and began writing conjugations on the board as if nothing had happened.

Fiona sat with pain burning her hands and rage coiling in her chest—not just for the strap or the insults, but for the shame that lived inside her, like a bruise that never healed.

Still, she would scrub harder and learn faster, and remember every word. Because soon she would leave this place, and when she did, no one would speak her mother's name with judgment and hatred again.

~ ~ ~

Later that evening, the kitchen was quiet except for the ticking of the clock above the spice cupboard and the clinks of Sister Bernadette washing up in the scullery. The girls had been fed, the floors scrubbed, and the bread set to rise for morning.

Fiona rubbed the salve into her palms as she sat at the corner table with a folded map spread before her. She'd found it tucked inside an old geography book and slipped it into her apron when no one was looking.

Isabel padded in and poured two cups of tea. She set one down beside Fiona and slid onto the bench. "What's that?"

"A map." Fiona tapped a spot on the page. "It's got all the rail lines." She tapped the word Syracuse.

Isabel leaned closer, brushing a strand of hair behind her ear. "Why Syracuse?"

"Aye, that's where they're sending me for a cooking placement. They need kitchen help." Her mouth twisted. "Ach! They're calling it a golden opportunity as though they don't know it's just another set of hands to scald."

"That's far." Isabel ran a finger over the map.

"Blathers. That's really far."

"I know."

Fiona traced the rail line with her finger, from Brooklyn through Albany, then west along the tracks. The line stretched like a vein across the state. Until now, her world had been row houses, kitchens, nuns with cold hands, and an orphan asylum. "I've never been on a train."

"You've barely even been out of the borough."

She nodded. "Aye, everything I know is here. This building and kitchen." She turned to Isabel suddenly. "What if I make a mistake and burn the sauce or drop the chicken?" She paused. "What if Sister Catherine's right?"

Isabel set her tea down. "Nae. She's not right!"

"You don't know that."

"Aye. I know you."

Fiona looked away. "She said I'd never be more than my mother. And sometimes…" She swallowed.

"I'm so scared she's right. That it's in my blood or that I'll end up alone, disgraced, and ruined."

Isabel took Fiona's hand. "Nae! You're not your mother's mistakes."

"She didn't make a mistake," Fiona whispered. "She tried to give me a life, and she was all I had. She sang to me and told me stories while she cooked supper. Even after the trial, even in jail…she wrote to me."

"Then why are you ashamed?"

Fiona didn't answer right away. "Because I loved her and tried to tell them the truth," she moaned, "but it still wasn't enough to save her."

"But it wasn't your job to save her."

They sat quietly until Sister Bernadette's humming carried from the scullery, and somewhere down the corridor, a girl coughed.

Isabel pointed at the map. "Then go to Syracuse, Fiona. Cook with all your heart, and be better than all of them. Not because you have to prove her wrong, but because that's how you keep your mother with you."

Fiona blinked, pressing her palms into her eyes. She swiped at her cheeks before folding the map, her movements painful from the welts. "I'm scared, Izzy," she said again, but shakier this time. "I know I am strong, and I've always been, but I'm scared to death."

"Aye, but you don't have to be unafraid," Isabel said. "You just have to get on the train."

Fiona smiled, the smallest tug at one corner of her mouth as fear took a back seat to hope—or maybe just the possibility of hope.

She would ride the train to the north and then west. She would carry the memory of her mother with her, and someday, she would make a name worth remembering.

The kitchen was almost dark when Isabel left, the coals banked low. A warm hush settled in the air, and suddenly, a clatter came from the scullery.

Sister Bernadette emerged, hands wringing a towel that no longer needed drying. Her round face flushed when she noticed Fiona. "Oh, sorry! I didn't mean to startle you."

Fiona shrugged and stepped to the stove. She poured herself the last of the tea left in the pot and leaned against the worktable. The space between them was easy and familiar.

Then Sister Bernadette said, "I heard what happened with Sister Catherine. She shouldn't have said those things. Not about your mother, and not about you."

Fiona stiffened and sipped the tea, even though it was tepid. She set the cup down with more force than intended. "It's fine. It's done."

"No, Fiona." Sister Bernadette gently patted the top of her hand. "It's not fine."
Really? Fiona's gaze shot to the kind nun.

Sister Bernadette flushed deeper, but she didn't look away. "She was cruel, and you stood there and took it—as you always do. But just because you can carry it doesn't mean you should have to."

Fiona stared at her, the words catching like brambles.

"You're strong," Sister Bernadette continued. "Stronger than any of us. The girls look up to you— they call you 'Mother' when they think no one's listening. Even I look up to you, and I'm supposed to be the nun."

That drew a laugh out of Fiona—more like a huff—but it was genuine.

Sister Bernadette smiled at that, then hesitated. "Can I tell you something?"

Fiona raised an eyebrow but nodded.

"I joined the order because I didn't know where else to go." Her hands fidgeted with the towel again. "I grew up in the St. Steven Orphanage. It wasn't a kind place, and I wasn't brave, not like you. I cried all the time and wet the bed until I was nine.

The older girls used to hide my shoes and tell me I'd never be chosen and that no one wanted a girl with a stutter and crooked teeth."

Fiona's brow furrowed as she whispered, "Oh, my goodness." She'd never imagined Sister Bernadette in such a state. She was always soft and kind with a gentle laughter as sweet as warm sugar.

"I remember Sister Agatha. She was the music teacher, and she'd let me stay behind after lessons. She said I had a 'sweet ear,' whatever that meant, and she made me feel seen for a little while." Sister Bernadette paused, her smile dimming with memory. "When I aged out, I had nothing. No skills, and no money, so I joined the sisters. I thought if I became one of them, I could be like Sister Agatha and help some girls the way she helped me."

Fiona smiled. "Aye. You already do."

Sister Bernadette blinked at her. "You think?"

"Aye! You're the one the wee ones run to, and you've helped me over and over."

Sister Bernadette bit her lip, eyes glimmering. Fiona smiled one of her rare smiles. "'Tis true that you panic when we run out of lard or when you burn the porridge. You're a hard worker and love to serve others."

That made Sister Bernadette laugh— awkward and grateful. "And you," she said, stepping closer, "are not your mother's shadow. You're a young woman with fire in her bones. You're sharp and steady, and you see everything. I know you're scared, Fiona, but that just means you care."

Fiona looked down at her hands—the red welts from earlier started to fade into aching ghosts. "Aye, but I've never been anywhere. Not beyond Brooklyn and never on a train. I might act as though I don't need anyone, but if I fail…"

"You won't."

"But if I do, there's no one waiting for me."

Sister Bernadette patted her arm. "Then come back here and become a nun if you're called to, or find Isabel. We're not much, but we are yours."

Fiona's throat tightened. She looked away, blinking. "Blathers! I've never had someone say that."

"Well," Sister Bernadette gave her a shy smile. "I pray you find much more affirmation in your future."

The kitchen fell silent again, and she no longer felt the chill of night. Fiona glanced once more at the folded map. She still didn't know what waited in Syracuse, but perhaps she didn't have to carry her fear alone.

And maybe the bravest thing she could do wasn't leaving. It was letting someone care.

CHAPTER 12

The next day, the scent of the medicinal combination of marigold and rosemary lingered in the air as Taryn crushed them under her pestle. Outside the window, the late-afternoon sun scattered a golden light through the tiny greenhouse's glass panes, painting streaks across the worn wooden floor. She liked the quiet here—the order and purpose where every leaf had a use, and every task mattered.

Sister Clare moved with grace, as always, matching the swish of her habit. "You're pressing too hard, child." Her Irish lilt wended around the words like music.

Taryn loosened her grip, though her jaw remained tight. She wasn't angry. Just always a little clenched, as if she let go for even a second, something might crack.

"We need this salve ready before supper," Sister Clare muttered. "Eliza's got a bad scrape from the well, and the herbs will be more effective if they are coaxed, not punished."

Taryn didn't answer, but her pounding stopped. Sister Clare had a way of saying things that weren't about herbs at all.

They worked for a while in a silence broken by the snip of scissors and the rustle of dried leaves. Then Sister Clare spoke with tenderness, as she often did, like slipping a stone into a still pond. "You're skilled, Taryn, and the girls trust you. So do I."

Taryn didn't look up. "Because I can bandage a wound?"

"Because you can see pain—and do something about it. You have a gift with the garden, with the sick, and even the scared. You calmed that young lad who helped in the garden when no one else could."
"He was just shivering, so I gave him mint tea."

"You wrapped your coat 'round him and sat with him 'til he stopped trembling. You don't give yourself enough credit."

Taryn shrugged, uncomfortable. She hated praise because praise felt like expectations, and expectations turned into pressure.

Sister Clare continued, her voice tender but firm. "You revived Maryanne when she collapsed. Not every girl your age could think clearly in a moment like that."

"Aye, I just did what you taught me."

"And you remembered in the panic. That's rare."

Taryn stared into the mortar, watching the crushed calendula blur. The scent reminded her of summer fields, the ones she and Annie used to run through before everything fell apart. Before Father left and Mother wasted away.

Sister Clare stood beside her now, brushing a lock of chestnut hair from Taryn's face. "You've tended to so many, lass. But I see how you hold yourself from others. You care for those who hurt but not for your own wounds."

Taryn swallowed hard. "I'm fine." "Nae, you're not."

There was no judgment in Sister Clare's tone.

Just truth. "You carry bitterness like a splinter in the soul. I see it when you flinch at kindness. When you close yourself off and when you set that jaw like armor."

Taryn clenched it tighter, as if to prove her right.

"I know pain." Sister Clare frowned. "I watched typhus take my whole family before I was eight. I was angry, too, but grief curdled into bitterness will hollow you out. You have to forgive— especially your sister."

Taryn's eyes snapped up, dark and stormy. "Annie didn't suffer the way I did. She got a home while I—"

"I know," Sister Clare interrupted. "Yes, Annie had the blessing of being adopted by the Barkers and you did not. They gave her nice things and tennis lessons and a home. But when Mrs. Barker died, Annie lost everything. She was rejected by Mr. Barker and sent back here. She lost a lot, too, Taryn, don't forget that. Holding onto that ache will hurt you more. Bitterness doesn't protect, my sweet lassie. It poisons."

Taryn looked away, blinking fast. Her throat felt tight. She hated this, and hated being seen. "I can't just forget."

"No one's asking you to," Sister Clare said. "But you can cut the bitterness out like a rotten root, before it spreads."

Silence settled between them again, heavier this time. Then Sister Clare placed a warm biscuit on the table. "Eat. You always think better after a bit of shortbread."

Taryn stared at it, then at Sister Clare. "You always carry biscuits."

Sister Clare grinned her typical half smile. "Just for the stubborn ones."

A reluctant twitch tugged at Taryn's lips. She didn't smile, but her jaw unclenched.

Maybe Sister Clare was right. Perhaps it was time to stop punishing the herbs—and herself.

~ ~ ~

By the time the bell rang for supper, the biscuit was long gone. Taryn had lingered in the greenhouse longer than she meant to, wiping down the pestle and straightening jars with more force than necessary. Sister Clare's words had nested behind her ribs, irritating and warming at the same time.

"Cut it out before it spreads." But she didn't know how.

The dining hall was already buzzing when she stepped inside, long tables crowded with girls and the clatter of spoons against bowls. She spotted Annie near the end, waving with that too-eager smile. The one that made Taryn feel strange inside, as though she was eleven again, watching Annie win over an adoptive family with charm, while Taryn just wanted someone to notice when she got every answer right.

She sat across from her twin, ladling stew into her bowl.

Annie's hazel eyes flitted to her. "Sister Clare said you helped Eliza today. She said you were gentle." Taryn shrugged. "She just tripped over a root. She'll be fine."

"I wish I could be like that," Annie said. "Calm in emergencies and useful in any situation."

"You're not useless," Taryn muttered, her gaze fixed on her spoon.

No one spoke for a few minutes. Then Annie asked, "Did you ever get my letters when I lived at the Barkers'?"

Taryn's spoon stopped halfway to her mouth. "What letters?"

Annie blinked. "I wrote you every fortnight after the split for almost a year."

Taryn set her spoon down, hard. "I never got a single one."

"I swear, Taryn, I sent them. I asked Mr. Barker to post them himself."

"And I'm supposed to believe that some businessman lost them?" Taryn's brows furrowed. "Or maybe you didn't bother writing at all."

Annie recoiled. "I did. I waited and waited for you to write back. I thought you hated me."

"I was here, under Sister Catherine's thumb," Taryn snapped. "Do you know what it was like here, without you, Annie? While you were learning embroidery and playing tennis?"

"I didn't choose where I was sent," Annie hissed.

"I didn't ask for a warm bed or a kind matron."

"But you got them, didn't you?" Taryn accused, and a few heads turned, but she didn't care.

Annie squeaked a whisper. "You think I wanted to be apart from you? I cried every night, and I begged to be sent back."

"But you stayed," Taryn spat. "You stayed safe and forgot me."

"I never forgot you!" Annie rose to her feet. "Even now, when you have stopped acting like my sister, I still care. I will always care."

The words hit like a slap as Taryn's chest burned, every part of her aching to say something crueler. To win the argument and shove the pain back where it belonged—inside Annie instead of her.

But then Sister Clare's voice echoed again in her mind. You carry bitterness like a splinter in the soul. Taryn bolted to her feet, her chair scraping back.

"Oh, just forget it," she said coldly. "It doesn't matter."

"It does," Annie whispered. "You just won't let it."

Taryn stormed out of the dining hall before she could cry. The corridor was quiet, lit only by the flickering oil sconces along the stone wall. Taryn's boots echoed as she walked, fast and aimless. Her fists were balled in her apron, and her throat was tight with tears she refused to release. She hated crying, for it made her weak, and she hated Annie even more for nearly making her do it.

Before she reached the back stairwell, someone called down the hall, "Taryn Burns. My office. Now, please."

She froze.

Sister Rose was never harsh, but her words landed as a distinct command.

Taryn turned and walked toward the door that loomed like a confessional. Inside, Sister Rose was seated behind her carved oak desk, hands folded atop a worn prayer book. Her pale blue eyes met Taryn's with unsettling calm.

Taryn didn't sit. "I didn't start it. If this is about dinner—"

"This is about your heart," Sister Rose interrupted. "Sit."

Taryn obeyed, her jaw set tight again.

Sister Rose studied her for a moment, her gaze piercing but not unkind. "You've built quite the fortress around yourself, haven't you?" Taryn didn't answer.

"I understand why. Some girls use silence as armor, and others use charm. You? You use control and blame."

Taryn stiffened. "I'm not like Annie."

"No," Sister Rose said. "You're not, and yet, you've made her the enemy."

Taryn swallowed her guilt. "She had an easy life while I…"

"Yes. She did, and you had a hard one. That's the truth, but not all of it."

Taryn blinked at her, caught off guard.

"The truth is," Rose continued, "your sister wrote to you, she wept for you, and she still aches for you. Yet you punish her, not because she hurt you, but because the world did, and she was spared."

Taryn opened her mouth and closed it.

Sister Rose stood and crossed to the window, hands clasped behind her back. "Bitterness is a blade that wounds the hand that holds it. You carry yours so tightly, it's started bleeding into everything you touch."

Taryn stared at the worn wood of the desk, tracing the grain with her finger. "She should've tried harder," she whispered.

"Perhaps," Sister Rose agreed. "But she was a child, and so were you. And now, you're almost grown. That means it's time to choose truth over anger, and love over pride."

Taryn's throat swelled. "I don't know how." Sister Rose returned to her chair. "Start small, and speak truth without rage. Ask questions instead of assuming answers, and tell her what you needed without making her pay for what she couldn't give." Taryn swallowed hard.

"She's not your enemy, Taryn. But bitterness will be if you let it stay."

After a long pause, Taryn gave a single nod, not more than a heartbeat.

Sister Rose smiled. "You may go."

Taryn stood and turned to leave, but at the door, she paused. "I don't think I can forgive her yet." "Then forgive what you can," Rose said, "and let the rest come later. But try every day."

Taryn stepped into the hall, her heart sore and her mind full. She didn't know how to face Annie, but maybe tomorrow she'd try.

~ ~ ~

The next morning came gray and hushed. Taryn was up before the bell, re-stocking salves and tinctures, needing the routine to ground her. But the words from Sister Rose kept looping.

"Speak truth without rage." That was easier said than done.

By midmorning, she'd almost talked herself out of it again. But then she caught sight of Annie across the courtyard—seated on the stone bench near the laundry steps, clutching a bit of mending in her lap and staring down at the thread as though it had betrayed her.

Taryn's chest tightened with the same twin-shaped pull she always tried to ignore. She crossed the yard before she could stop herself.

Annie looked up when she heard the steps. Her eyes were cautious, red-rimmed, but hopeful, and that made it worse.

"I'm not here to fight." Taryn held up her hands. Annie nodded. "Okay."

Taryn stood, her gaze on the hedge behind her sister's head. "I'm still mad, and I don't know if that's fair or not, but it's what I feel."

Annie nodded again, more slowly. "Okay." "I never got the letters," Taryn said. "And maybe that wasn't your fault. But I needed someone, and you weren't there."

"I know," Annie whispered.

Taryn's voice wobbled for half a second. "And it hurt."

For a moment, neither of them spoke. Then Annie's squeaked out, "I wish I could go back and have tried harder, but I didn't know how much you were hurting."

"You still don't." It didn't come out cruel, at least. "I want to understand, even if you're still mad."

Taryn snapped her gaze toward her. The same eyes and face as her own, but softer. "I'm not ready, but I don't want to lose you again."

Annie held back choking emotion. "Then let's not."

Taryn nodded, slow and uncertain, and sat on the bench, but not too close.

It wasn't a truce, but it was a start.

CHAPTER 13

Cassie struck the match with a steady hand, shielding the tiny flame from the draft in the chapel's east wall. The third candle—rose-colored, unlike the others—stood between the flickering purple ones, expectant and solemn.

Joy. Rejoice. What does that mean for us as orphans?

The wick caught, a small flare of light flaring up before settling into a flickering glow. Cassie adjusted her spectacles and bit her bottom lip. What could she say, especially now that Sister Rose summoned all the girls, big and small, to join the meeting?

The idea of joy seemed too cheerful for a concept so often misused. People talked of it as if it were just a feeling or as if one simply had to wait until it floated in on a breeze of good weather or kind words.

She fisted her writing hand, self-conscious of the ink smudge she'd half scrubbed from her finger that Mouser had caused by distracting her with his yowling the entire time as she prepared her notes. Now, perched near the altar, the fool cat let out a low, approving purr as if he'd been the one to compose her devotion.

Grateful that Sister Rose allowed the comforting animal in the chapel, Cassie stepped to the front, her notebook cradled in her palm. Sister Rose gave her a slight nod from the pews, and Cassie straightened her shoulders.

She read her notes, precise and steady.

"Nehemiah 8:10 says, 'Neither be ye sorry, for the joy of the Lord is your strength.'" She paused, letting the words settle with no dramatics or clever anecdotes. Just Scripture, clean and direct like a bookkeeping ledger.

She cleared her throat. "I'm beginning to understand that joy is not about feelings. It's a choice that isn't made in laughter or ease. In Nehemiah's day, the people were exhausted and scared and unsure of their future just like us, but they chose to rejoice in their difficult situations."

Cassie glanced down at her notes, though she knew them by heart. She had recited them twice while copying inventory numbers and again while drying the dishes.

"We won't always feel joyful," she said, glancing toward the younger girls in the front pew— some squirming, some curious, and some not quite awake. "But we can choose joy the same way we choose to get up in the morning or to do what is right, even when it's hard."

She hesitated for just a moment, not because she didn't know what came next, but because it felt too close to her present condition. "I don't know what the journey ahead will look like for you or for me, but we can find joy in each day. If the Lord is in it, that's enough."

Cassie closed the notebook with a snap and returned to her seat, her steps tapping on the old stone floor. She didn't look to see if the girls understood, and she didn't need applause.

Mouser bumped his head against her ankle, so she reached down, gave his ears a scratch, and whispered, "You'll have to write next week's if you're going to critique this one."

Sister Rose moved to the front with the gentle authority that made even the youngest girls sit up straighter. "I want to tell you something about where I came from." Sister Rose's gaze was warm but full of gravity. She unpinned the rose pin she wore from her lapel and held it in her open palm.

Cassie had noticed it often—five petals, simple and elegant, but forged in silver—though she'd never asked about it.

"The Irish rose is not a flower you'll find in gardens," Sister Rose said. "It grows in the wild Irish places on rocky soil with coastal winds and harsh winters. And still, it blooms year after year, reaching its roots deep and secure."

The room fell into a reverent hush. Even Mouser seemed to still. "The Irish rose is not known for its beauty, the way English roses are, but it endures through time. It refuses to give in and is stubborn and resilient, and that's why I wear it."

Cassie made a quick note of the nun's words in the margin of her notebook, though she wasn't sure why. The words weren't numbers or statistics, but there was something important in them, and she found herself leaning forward.

"My family came from Cork." Sister Rose's tone reflected melancholy. "We came here with empty pockets and meaningless names, scraping by in poor neighborhoods with menfolk who worked themselves to death just to survive. We were called Micks and lessthan, and we were told we didn't belong."

She paused and returned to her story with steel behind the softness. "But we endured. We worked and the children were educated. We held our heads up, even in places where no one wanted us, and we carried with us the memory of what it meant to keep faith and joy alive when the world offered us none. And so, I know. I understand." She lifted her hand to show them the silver pin. "This rose is not for show. It is not a piece of fancy jewelry but a reflection of the inner soul, a symbol of strength."

Cassie swallowed, surprised by the lump in her throat. She didn't cry and hadn't—not since the fever took her parents and left her to find security in arithmetic and bookkeeping and the safety of structure.

Sister Rose's kind gaze landed on her, and for a moment, Cassie felt as if the whole chapel faded into a hushed solemnity. "Cassie, what you said about joy is not just a nice thought. Joy is our inheritance, and we choose joy because it has always been the mark of survivors. That is what we Irish are—and who each of you are."

Cassie gave a single nod to acknowledge she understood. Several girls whispered behind her, but she didn't turn around.

Sister Rose addressed the rest of the girls. "Each of you carries something you did not ask for. You've had hard beginnings and have endured grief no child should ever have to experience. But you are not the sum of what has happened to you. Instead, you are what you choose to do in response those challenges. Let joy be your strength and faith be the roots that sink deep and strong. Let the wild Irish rose bloom in your life, even in the hard soil of heartache and difficulties."

The small flame of the joy candle flickered a warm glow across the chapel as Cassie grasped those thoughts and held them tight. She didn't need to write that part down, for she had already recorded it in her mind and even deeper in her heart.

As the final echoes of Sister Rose's words faded, a small hand shot up from the front pew. From the corner of her eye, Cassie recognized the determined posture even before she saw the face.

Gloria always had a question—often two— and none of them were rhetorical.
Sister Rose smiled. "Yes, Gloria?"

The girl stood, her light-brown braids bouncing with the motion. "If the Irish rose grows in hard places, does that mean we're like that, too, since we come from hard places?"

A few of the younger girls turned to look at her, and one elbowed her friend for whispering.

Sister Rose didn't answer right away. She stepped closer to the pews, her skirts rustling, the silver rose in her hand catching the candlelight. "Yes, Gloria," she said. "That's what I mean, thank you. God sometimes allows us to be planted in hard soil so our roots grow deep. That way, when true joy blooms, it's real and not fragile like the happy- faced joy that lasts but for a moment. You, my children, have earned that deep and lasting joy, and it can become a foundation for your whole life."

Cassie tapped her journal, her fingers tracing the margin of her notes. Did she have deep roots like the sister said? She huffed. It was the sort of thing Sister Catherine would scoff at as sentimental nonsense.

Another hand went up. This time, it belonged to Isabel, who rarely spoke aloud in chapel. Cassie raised an eyebrow. This should be good.

"Yes, Isabel?"

Isabel bit her lip. "But what if you don't feel joyful? Not ever, and what if you try to find joy and it still doesn't work?"

Cassie's brow furrowed at Isabel's trembling and the flicker of panic in the girl's dark eyes as soon as the words were out, as though Isabel regretted giving them life. A pang of sympathy surged through Cassie, for her friend took a risk by saying something honest in front of others.

Sister Rose tilted her chin. "That's a very brave question, and the truth is, you won't always feel joy. Just as you won't always feel brave or kind or patient or obedient. But that doesn't mean those things aren't growing inside you." She motioned toward the candle, the rose-colored one glowing bright. "That's why we light the candles. It's not because we feel joyful, but because we are practicing joy and hope and peace, just like we are building muscles."

A murmur of understanding traveled among the girls. Some were nodding, and Isabel looked relieved, though still a little pale.

It was time for Cassie to be brave too. She hesitated, then lifted her hand. "So, joy is a discipline," she said aloud, more to herself than the room. "A decision and not an emotion?"

A few heads swiveled toward her in surprise since Cassie wasn't often the one to speak during chapel unless correcting a Latin conjugation. Heat rose in her cheeks, but she didn't look away.

Sister Rose offered a gentle smile that suggested she'd been hoping someone would say just that. "Yes, Cassie. It's like learning the discipline of keeping books accurately or rising early or telling the truth. Joy can be practiced even when it's difficult."

Another hand shot up. It was Gloria again, her round baby face and gentle green eyes hopeful. "Is your rose pin magical?" she asked Sister Rose. "I mean, if you wear it, will it make you brave and joyful?"

The older girls giggled, but Sister Rose didn't. She leaned down so she was eye-level with her. "No, sweet girl, it's not magic. It is a reminder of something real, and I wear it to remember who I am, and Whom I serve." She tapped her heart. "The rose doesn't make me brave, but it reminds me to choose courage and joy no matter what comes my way."

Cassie stared at the pin again. She had once assumed Sister Rose wore it out of nostalgia or tradition. She hadn't considered that the pin might be an anchor for her.

A peaceful silence followed, like the quiet that comes after a snowfall.

Sister Rose scanned the girls one last time. "Any more questions?"

No hands went up this time. Mouser let out a grumpy yowl that echoed off the stone.

Cassie smirked. "I think that was a no," she said under her breath.

Sister Rose chuckled, then raised her hand in dismissal. "Then go in peace, girls, and let joy go with you."

Cassie lingered, rubbing the spine of her notebook. Her mind allocated Sister Rose's words to something important, like footnotes in the margin of her ever-growing ledger.

She'd have to find a way to write all this down, and not just the facts but the depth of it. Joy, it seemed, was not only strength—it was a strategy for life, a deliberate act of preservation and protection— and she intended to practice it.

CHAPTER 14

Sister Rose's announcement cut through the chatter.

"Taryn. Annie. Fiona. Gloria. Isabel. Vivian. Cassie. Stay in the chapel, please."

Mouser stayed, too, though his tail flicked in short, annoyed lashes.

Taryn sighed, plunked down and watched the stream of girls in uniforms move. The benches creaked as the younger girls filed out in twos and threes, the usual post-assembly chatter following them into the hallway.

Around her, the other six shifted and exchanged glances. Taryn cataloged their anticipation, imagining what each one thought, and she was quite certain she was right.

Annie's hazel-green eyes were already shiny, which was ridiculous considering nothing had happened yet. Cassie pushed her spectacles up on her nose and closed her notebook with precision, fingers resting on the worn cover as though it was a shield. Vivian swiped at her wild red hair with restless confidence. Isabel didn't so much as blink—she held that statue-still posture that shouted that control was a choice. Gloria blinked as she unraveled a loose thread, slow and methodical, as though her sleeve's destruction might keep her invisible.

Finally, Mouser slid away with a flick of his tail, silent as a shadow. The sensible animal seemed to know when it was time to skedaddle.

Once the girls settled back down in their seats, Sister Rose smiled, retrieved a small wooden box from behind the altar, and set it on the front pew. All seven of them leaned in, though not enough to seem eager.

"As you know," Sister Rose began, "in less than a month, you'll be off to your assigned placements and apprenticeships, and into the world beyond these walls."

Taryn huffed. To their assigned placements— as though they were pawns in some chess game, positioned with intention instead of shoved wherever there was space. Like hers, emptying bedpans and cleaning soiled sheets for old people. Those jobs were for aides. She wanted to be a real nurse at a real hospital—or possibly be trained at a Nightingale Training School one day. Fat chance for that.

"I won't give you long speeches," she continued, "but I want to mark this moment. To give you something that speaks of who you are—and who you're becoming."

She opened the box. Inside, nestled in worn velvet, lay seven tin lockets—heart shaped, simple, and engraved with a five-petaled rose. The design was plain enough to be dismissed by anyone not looking for symbolism, which meant it had been chosen with care. They weren't quite beautiful. Instead, they seemed like a keepsake, which made them even more interesting.

Sister Rose waited for their attention to return to her, pointing to the rose on the locket. "This rose is a symbol of choosing joy and strength in hard places, of perseverance, and of blooming even when the soil is dry and rocky."

Taryn huffed. Joy in hard places? That's the kind of thing people said when they couldn't change anything, but there was a part of her that wanted to believe it could be real. She wanted to believe that her hard places could become beautiful and strong like the fragrant flowers that also held those prickly thorns. She'd seen roses just a few times as she passed by a floral shop in the summertime. She'd stopped to smell them, to touch their velvety petals— until the shopkeeper slapped her hand and shooed her away, calling her a filthy street urchin.

Sister Rose interrupted her musings as, one by one, she gave each girl her necklace. "Isabel—for your steadiness and artistic talent." Isabel smiled.

"Gloria—for your tenderness and angelic voice."

Taryn pursed her lips. Predictable, since Gloria's heart bled for anyone who looked the least bit wounded. Still, maybe the world needed people like that.

"Vivian—for your courage and leadership."

Vivian grinned and said something about 'except when it comes to jelly beans.'

Taryn almost smiled at that.

"Fiona—for your caring heart and faithful service."

Fiona took her gift like someone receiving a burden she'd already decided to carry.

"Annie—for your warmth and kindness."

Annie cradled her necklace in both hands as though it was breakable. Taryn rolled her eyes.

Then Sister Rose looked at her. "Taryn, for your keen mind. But also, for your heart, which I pray, you will one day trust again and know how precious it is."

Taryn didn't appreciate the way that last part hit her, like a hand knocking on a door she'd nailed shut so long ago. Something in her chest twisted, so she pocketed the locket before anyone could see her reaction.

Cassie's came last. Sister Rose placed it in her open palm. "For your integrity and meticulous nature."

Cassie took it without a fuss as though she already knew what the nun would say.

When it was done, the others turned their lockets over, tracing petals and testing chains. But Taryn kept hers where it was, the metal warming against her palm in her pocket.

Trust and joy. Blooming in hard soil.

They were all fine words, but she'd learned long ago that difficult places didn't change just because someone wanted them to.

Sister Rose's final words exhorted them solemnly. "Wear it or don't, but remember what it means. You are not what the world has called you, and you are more than what you lost."

Taryn had heard variations of the speech before with different words but with the same empty promise. The symbol wasn't enough, and for her, the words fell flat.

The chapel grew silent. The joy candle flickered as though it was trying not to burn out, reminding her, too much, of herself. Yet, could this be a new beginning for her? A symbol like this should've seemed empty, but some small, traitorous part of her wanted to believe that new beginnings were still possible.

The poignant moment dissolved as soon as they left the chapel. Vivian was the first to break the hush, flipping her locket over and squinting at the engraving.

"This tin is thin, so these lockets will scratch and bend easily. We'll have to keep them wrapped in something to protect them."

"Aye, or polish them," Isabel suggested. "You can use a bit of vinegar and a soft cloth."

Annie cradled hers like a rare jewel. "Maybe Sister Agnes can show us how to sew little pouches for them. That way we can keep them—"

"Oh, for heaven's sake!" Taryn cut in, sarcasm tainting her words. "It's a piece of tin, not the crown jewels."

Her words dropped like a stone in a bucket. Gloria furrowed her brow, her lips pressed tight. Fiona kept walking, a loud huff trailing behind her. Vivian muttered, "Somebody woke up on the wrong side of the bed…again."

Taryn didn't care—or at least, she told herself she didn't.

By the time they reached the candle-dim dormitory, Annie and Gloria were still murmuring about proper storage options as Fiona offered the occasional practical suggestion on how to keep the lockets safe.

Taryn slipped into her corner of the room, opened the shared cupboard, and shoved the locket to the very back. It was out of sight and out of the way, where it would stay until she could deal with its implications—alone.

She closed the cupboard door harder than necessary, and a few heads turned her way. Thanks to her cynical attitude, she'd dampened the girls' excitement yet again. Well, they could waste their energy on keeping the lockets safe as if that would make its meaning last. Taryn knew better. Things, especially symbolic things, got broken and tarnished or were taken away, so she'd rather be done with the sentimental now rather than watch it be lost to her.

By lights-out, the room had settled into its usual rhythm—the rustle of blankets, muffled coughs, and the faint creak of floorboards as someone shifted in their sleep. The faint sweetness of drying laundry hung thick on the air.

Taryn lay on her back, her eyes open in the dark. The familiar ceiling beams cut shadowy lines above her. She could still hear the muffled echo of the earlier chatter—Annie insisting her locket would stay by her bed so she could see it first thing every morning, and Vivian joking that she'd pawn hers for biscuits if she got hungry enough.

Taryn rolled onto her side, away from the sound of Annie's soft breathing. The cupboard stood across from her bed where, behind the folded sweater, the locket hid where she'd shoved it. She imagined it lying there, petals pressed flat into the metal, waiting for her— and the thought annoyed her.

No! That blasted piece of jewelry wasn't anything special, and the world didn't care how much you polished something, because it would take it from you, anyway. Even so, its presence throbbed like a splinter under her skin—small enough to ignore but impossible to forget. Yet, part of her liked knowing it waited there. But that was no one's business.

She tried to will herself toward sleep. But in the quiet, Sister Rose's words slipped back uninvited. "For your heart, which I pray, you will one day trust again and know how precious it is."

Taryn exhaled a heavy sigh.

~ ~ ~

When morning came with the usual bedsprings groaning, boots hitting the floor, and someone mumbling about cold water, Taryn sat on the edge of her bed, tying her laces with precise, deliberate pulls.

Gloria drifted past her and stopped just short at their shared cupboard. She opened the cupboard door, and her hand hovered for a second before she pulled it back as though she'd touched something hot.

Taryn snapped her gaze up. "What?"

"Why hide the locket?" Gloria whispered as if speaking the words too loudly might make the locket vanish. "At the very back behind everything." Her tone wasn't accusing, just surprised.

Taryn sucked in a breath and held it as a couple of the others glanced over at them. Heat pricked at her collar, but she kept her face passive. "I didn't want it getting scratched."

Gloria's brow knit, but she nodded. "Aye. That's smart. I just thought maybe you'd want to wear it like the rest of us."

Taryn yanked the second lace tight enough to creak. "It's not some fine jewelry. It's a cheap piece of tin on a chain, and wearing it won't solve anything."

Vivian, buttoning her uniform across the room, smirked. "Oh, aren't you just full of sunshine again today." It wasn't a question.

Taryn ignored the comment as she stood, and Gloria stepped away, a clean apron in her hand. Taryn shut the cupboard door with determination, too quiet to be a slam, but final all the same.

Gloria drifted away, and the moment dissolved into the clatter of girls finishing their morning routines. Still, the cupboard's shadow on the floorboards seemed darker than usual, as though it was guarding something.

But before Taryn left, she brushed her fingers across the cupboard door.

Maybe she'd deal with it soon.

CHAPTER 15

The evening after they received their lockets, Isabel gathered the girls together for a special meeting. She'd done it almost without thinking—just a gentle suggestion to meet in the attic after supper, her tone casual enough to avoid suspicion. But in truth, she'd needed time alone with them and didn't want Sister Catherine to interrupt them.

The attic smelled of cedar and dust, while the girls sat in a small circle on the worn rug, their knees touching now and then in the flicker of the single oil lamp. Outside, the wind scraped at the eaves, adding to the eerie atmosphere.

Isabel began the conversation, her words almost swallowed by the hush. "Now that it's been a few days, how are you all feeling about your future? Tomorrow is one day closer to the end of our time together." She gave a crooked smile. "And it feels as though we're being scattered like snowflakes across New York State." They laughed, but it felt brittle.

Fiona spoke next, her hands knotted in her lap. "Aye, I reckon I'll be leaving you first to become head cook." She gave a huff. "Head cook. Blathers! Don't they know I've only ever made bread and stew and oatmeal by myself? And I've never been in charge of a kitchen."

"Aye, but what about last winter when Sister Bernadette had the flu?" Isabel encouraged. "You did a fine job then, so I'm sure you'll make great work of it. You know everything about food, and we've never had a bad meal when you prepared it."

"Thanks, but I fear they'll soon discover how little I know. If I fail…"

Vivian leaned back on her palms. "I understand, Fiona. I'm not ready to be a nanny's assistant to four children. Besides, the letter said their mother is strict. I read the letter twice. She underlined obedience three times."

"Four children?" Cassie winced, her high forehead crinkling. "They'll test you, to be sure. But you've dealt with several of the little dickens from downstairs, and you've won over each one of them."

Vivian's mouth twitched, but she waved away the concerns. "I'll try my best, and if I survive, I'll send word to each of you."

Cassie slipped off her spectacles. "How can I do books for Henry Heath's manufacturing offices in Manhattan? I'll be working with businessmen, counting bolts of cloth—or who knows what—until my eyes cross. That's way different than doing Sister Rose's books."

Isabel smiled but imagined Cassie trapped in an airless storeroom, longing for the orphan noise. "Aye. It's honest work, Cassie, and a prime place for advancement."

"The thought of being a dresser and assistant to a lady's maid at the Buckingham Hotel—with continual pressure to do things right all the time—makes me queasy." The way Annie sat so primly and smoothed her skirt contrasted with her words.

Taryn harrumphed. "I'll be stuck in a stuffy, stinky Brooklyn almshouse with the elderly and infirm dying all around me." She swallowed. "Becoming a real nurse is what I want to do, but not this."

Next came Gloria, who seemed almost embarrassed to speak up. "I admit it. I'm glad I'm staying here to help Sister Agnes teach the younger girls, and help lead music and choir." She shrugged her shoulders, as if apologizing for not having to leave.

The girls murmured agreement before Cassie asked, "And you, Isabel?"

She shrugged. "Oh blathers. I'm just not sure if I can live up to the high expectations of being a proper scribe, copying important documents at a legal office, for heaven's sake."

They all sat silent for a long moment, each girl turning inward, their faces lit by the lamp, their shadows wavering like uneasy ghosts. This might be the last time they were all together like this. The sad thought settled in Isabel's chest, heavy and certain. Outside, the wind rattled the shingles again, but in the attic, their circle held steady, like a stubborn light against the dark.

"We say we'll remember our time together, but will we?" Fiona glanced around the circle, pointing toward the frosty window. "Once we're all out there, working for strangers, do you think we'll have time to write letters? Or will we just fade from each other's lives forever?"

"That's a mighty grim thought," Cassie muttered.

"It's an honest one," Fiona shot back. "We've seen it before. Girls leave, and we never hear from them again."

"That's because some of them don't want to be reminded of this place," Vivian motioned to the box of letters in the corner. "But we can be different. After all, we're the Irish Rose sisters, aren't we?"

Annie, prim as ever, lifted her chin. "Not everyone wants to carry the past around like a weight, Fiona. Sometimes you have to set it down if you want to walk forward."

"That's easy for you to say when you're going to some fine hotel," Taryn snapped. "You'll be dressing ladies in silk while I'm cleaning bedpans."

Annie flushed. "I didn't choose where I will be sent."

"No," Taryn's tone held a sarcastic tone. "But don't pretend you wouldn't choose it if you could. Just like before."

The air thickened, like a shroud surrounding them. Isabel wanted to step in and stop the twins, but those words had been simmering for months.

Gloria cleared her throat, her eyes tearing. "We're all nervous and scared, but it shouldn't tear us apart." She hesitated, looking down. "And yes, I know I'm the only one staying here, so I have the least to fear or criticize."

"You think staying's easier?" Cassie laughed, slipping off her spectacles. "You'll still be under the sisters' thumbs, especially Sister Catherine's, and we'll be out in the real world."

"That's not always better." Isabel's words slipped out before she could stop them. "The 'real world' doesn't notice or care if you're tired or sad or sick or cold." Silence settled again, but this time, it wasn't comfortable.

From below, the bell rang for evening prayers, yet none of them moved. Isabel's heart beat faster—not from fear of being caught, but from the sudden knowledge that they would all be carrying something heavier than suitcases when they left. Whether they saw each other again or not, if this bickering and these comparisons continued, it might be the last time they saw each other as friends. Their sister circle seemed to be splintering before them. But how could she stop it?

A floorboard creaked below. At first, Isabel thought it was the wind, but then came the echo of slow, deliberate steps on the attic stairs. Every girl froze, the lamplight too bright and their circle too loud even in its stillness.

The door swung open. Sister Catherine filled the doorway, her severe posture making her look scarier than usual. Her icy glare swept over them—seven girls caught like mice in a trap.

"What," she said, her scorn low and sharp as a knitting needle, "is the meaning of this?"

No one spoke. Isabel felt her own pulse in her throat.

"You were instructed to go to your room after dinner," Sister Catherine scolded. "Not to consort like hoodlums in forbidden places."

"The attic is not forbidden," Cassie blurted, putting her spectacles back on.

The sister's gaze snapped to her. "You will not speak unless asked."

Cassie's mouth clamped shut.

"We were just..." Isabel began, but Sister Catherine cut her off with a raised hand.

"I do not care for your—or any of your—excuses, Isabel." The way she said her name made Isabel feel smaller than she had in years. "Seven young women conspiring in an attic is not harmless. It is rebellion, and rebellion must be corrected before it infects others."

She stepped back and gestured for them to proceed downstairs. The girls filed past her in silence, the creak of the steps louder under their weighted steps. Sister Catherine led them to the cold schoolroom and stood at the front, hands clasped. She pointed to the chalkboard. "Each of you will copy the first two chapters of your catechism before you go to bed. In Latin."

Fiona made a small groan of protest but swallowed it.

"And," the Sister added, "none of you will whisper a word for the rest of the evening. Not one word or noise—or you'll get the strap." Gloria swallowed.

Sister Catherine's gaze softened just a fraction, but then it was gone. "You must always remember that discipline is not cruel. It is preparation for the world. Out there, mistakes have consequences much graver than a simple writing assignment."

She took a seat at her desk and waited for each girl to take her place at the slate board that took up the width of two walls. "Begin now, and write small enough for everyone to complete their work in the space allocated. And remember, not a sound except the squeak of the chalk."

Isabel began writing, her fingers cold. The weight of the other girls' angst around her almost sucked the air from the room. They'd lost the warm circle of earlier, but the seven sisters were still bound together by the scratch of chalk on a board.

Well, Sister Catherine was wrong! Rebellion wasn't always a sickness to be stamped out. Sometimes, it was the only way to survive, and live she would. She wrote and wrote, along with the others, until her hand cramped, the room cold enough to make her breath float in the lamplight. The girls stayed silent save the steady scrape of chalk and the occasional rustle of skirts as someone turned to find the next line to write.

Isabel continued her work, her cramped handwriting marching across the board. But after the first few paragraphs, her eyes began to blur. Sister Catherine seemed deep in the book she was reading—or almost asleep—so she risked a glance around to the others.

Cassie caught Isabel's gaze from two feet away, lifting one eyebrow in a silent, exaggerated 'really'? The expression made Isabel fight a smirk.

Annie, straight-backed and proper even in punishment, shifted the chalk to write in tiny loops.

Fiona, nearest the door, mouthed something Isabel couldn't quite catch. She tried again. "Tonight. Attic."

Isabel's pulse quickened—not with fear this time, but with hope.

The others were watching too. Taryn, who'd been so tense earlier, offered the smallest nod.

Gloria kept her head down, but her lips curved in the faintest smile, and Vivian's chalk scratched brisk and purposeful, as if she were already planning the words she'd share later.

It was nothing dramatic. No grand speech or bold act. Just seven girls, cold and sad, promising, without a word, that Sister Catherine's scolding wouldn't be the last word.

Then, Sister Catherine's head lifted, the rustle of her veil breaking the hush. "Enough! Do you think I don't see you whispering with your eyes? If one of you falters, you'll all begin again."

She stood, hands on her hips. "In fact, you will write the next two chapters as well. Every line. Without flourish. And you'll keep at it until you stop your rebelliousness."

A faint groan escaped Gloria. Cassie shifted, her jaw tight, but no one dared protest aloud. The chalk began again—scritch, scratch, scritch—faster now, though Isabel's hand ached.

Sister Catherine's condemning gaze could strip the air from their lungs, but a camaraderie remained.

Annie passed Isabel a new piece of chalk with a fleeting brush of fingers, almost a squeeze of reassurance. Fiona misspelled a word, earning them another hissed correction.

The punishment stretched on and on until their wrists cramped and their breath came shallow in the frigid air. Sister Catherine sat straight-backed, her narrowed glare never leaving them now, watching for cracks as she ensured silence would remain their punishing prison.

The camaraderie strengthened, unseen but unbreakable. Each girl embraced it, small and secret, like a tiny candle cupped in the palm.

When at last they were dismissed, filing out in rigid order, the echo of chalk scratching on the board still clung to Isabel's ears.

But the special connection between them remained—a stubborn thread tying them together.

CHAPTER 16

The evening after the chalkboard punishment, the chapel's candlelight tossed shadows that seemed to flicker in rhythm with Annie's heartbeat. The warmth of their sister session in the attic failed to steady her as she stood at the edge of the stage for one more pageant practice, her fingers twisting the ends of her braids until they frayed.

Across the room, Taryn moved like a soldier—every step measured, every gesture precise. Not a hair out of place in that crown-braid or a hint that she cared.

Two nights had passed since their quarrel. To Annie, it felt like two winters stacked on top of each other. The silence between them pressed heavier than any stone wall, and she couldn't bear it anymore. She needed to try to make amends.

As the girls settled into their places, Annie stepped close to her twin. Her throat ached and she tilted her face toward the rafters as though the courage she lacked might drift down from heaven itself. "Taryn, I can't stand this. We're family. Twins are supposed to be together and love each other. Please…can't we…"

Taryn turned. Her fists were tight, her lips pressed flat, and her glower sparked fire.

Annie's stomach knotted. She knew that look, that silent storm that gathered before it broke. Then Mouser padded between them, black fur gleaming, tail swaying as if to brush away the tension. Annie's heart leapt with relief, for Mouser always lightened things. She bent, ready to scoop him up.

But before she could, Taryn's kick landed hard, sending Mouser skittering with a pained yowl into the shadows.

Gasps filled the chapel, and Sister Clare barked Taryn's name.

Annie froze, and every vein in her body went cold. She had felt that blow as if it had struck her own ribs. "Taryn!" she cried, the name breaking out of her before she could catch it. "How could you?"

Tears fell hot, spilling down her cheeks, blurring Taryn into something unrecognizable—her twin, yet a stranger. Annie's chest throbbed with grief, not just for Mouser, but for the widening chasm between them.

And then she saw it—a flicker in Taryn's face, the tiniest fracture in that hard, unyielding mask. Grief, regret, or maybe both, but it was gone as soon as it came, swallowed by the steel walls Taryn built around herself. She turned away, arms locked across her chest.

Annie reached out, her hand trembling. "You don't have to fight me, Taryn. I'm not the enemy."

But her words fell into silence, echoing like unanswered prayers. Taryn didn't move or speak— she just took a small step away from Annie, glaring.

Annie stood there, her heart breaking to realize that the one she wanted most to comfort was the one who pushed her farthest away.

A small figure hurried past her. Gloria slipped to the shadows where Mouser had fled. The girl began to hum, tender and broken, a tune Annie herself often turned to when her nerves trembled.

"Ach! Poor wee kitty. I love you." Gloria whispered in her lilting Irish, crouching low. Mouser reappeared, slinking from the corner, his fur bristled. Gloria's round face glowed with sympathy as she held out her arms. "Come now, you've done nothin' wrong."

The tomcat pressed against her, his jet-black coat stark against her simple navy dress. She picked him up and stroked him, murmuring comfort as if speaking to a child.

Then Gloria turned, her light green glare flashing toward Taryn. The humming stopped. "Shame on you, Taryn Burns!" Her words trembled with emotion. "Kickin' an innocent creature. What's come over you? I thought you had a heart."

The words hung in the chapel, heavier than the incense smoke. Taryn flinched as though struck, her fists loosening at her sides. She glanced at Annie, then at Gloria, and then down at the stone floor.

"I…" Taryn's voice cracked, and for a moment, she looked younger than her fourteen years. "I'm sorry."

The apology was real. Annie felt it, but it was too small to fill the silence, and too late to erase the offense.

Around them, the other girls stared, plainly disappointed. Even Sister Clare shook her head, muttering beneath her breath.

Taryn stood alone, apology still echoing, yet no one stepped forward to accept it. The crown-braid gleamed beneath the candlelight, tight as the walls she'd built around herself.

Annie's chest ached. She wanted to run to her twin, to forgive and lessen the blow. But she couldn't, not when Mouser had been kicked and not when everyone's scowl brimmed with judgment. Even she couldn't shake her own disappointment.

Beside her, Gloria cradled Mouser in her arms, the cat purring, soothed by her touch. She rocked him, humming again, casting one last look of reproach at Taryn before turning away.

Annie stood between them—her sister's shame on one side and Gloria's compassion on the other, and she felt more torn than ever.

An hour later, the dormitory was quiet except for the wind rattling the shutters. The girls lay in their narrow beds lining the stone wall, the candle snuffed, the air cold and damp. Annie stared up into the dark, her heart restless.

She could still hear Mouser's cry, still see Gloria's hurt expression, still feel the sting of disappointment circling Taryn like a noose. The image of her sister's bowed head—that brief crack in her armor—wouldn't leave her mind.

Annie pressed her palms together over her chest. She's my twin. My own blood. How can I not go and help her?

She slipped from her bed. The cold floor bit at her bare feet as she padded across to where Taryn lay curled, her braid uncoiled now, her hair spread across the pillow like a dark crown undone. In repose, she looked softer, the hard edges blurred.

But Annie knew she wasn't asleep. The faint stiffness in her shoulders and the way her fists pressed the blanket betrayed the fact that Taryn was awake, pretending.

Annie knelt beside her. For a long moment, she said nothing and breathed in the silence. Then she whispered, "Taryn…I forgive you." Her words trembled, but they carried the truth.

Taryn shifted, her face turning toward Annie. In the faint moonlight, her twin's eyes glistened, wide and startled, as if she hadn't expected grace, just more judgment. Her lips parted, but no words came.

Annie reached for her hand, prying it open from its fist. Her own slim fingers slid inside. "We must always stand together," she murmured. "Not apart."

For a tiny moment, Taryn didn't respond. Then her grip tightened, fierce and trembling. A single tear slipped free down her cheek, catching the moonlight before disappearing into the pillow.

Annie smiled, and the ache in her chest eased. It wasn't gone, but it was gentler now. Whatever storms still waited for them, she had chosen.

Chosen love. Chosen forgiveness. And for the first time in days, she felt hope flicker in the darkness.

~ ~ ~

When the pale morning light spilled through the dormitory windows, it washed over the girls as they bustled into their chores. The sting of the previous night's rehearsal still lingered, a shadow no one wanted to name. Mouser prowled at the edge of the room, slipping close to Gloria's skirts.

Annie hovered near Taryn, protective in a quiet way. Her forgiveness had been whispered in the dark, a fragile truce only the two of them shared. But she was certain her sister still felt the weight of every disapproving eye.

Then Vivian approached. She was the steady one, her freckles and dimples and wild coppery hair easing the ire from the night before. Today she carried something small cupped in her hands. Her eyes—clear as the lake on a windless morning— rested on Taryn.

"I made this for you," Vivian held out the gift.

Taryn blinked, clearly uncertain. She didn't trust gifts, not when they came across like pity. But Vivian unfolded her palm to reveal a tiny hand-sewn heart, its seams neat and strong against the straw stuffing. In red thread, words were stitched across it—Hope. Peace. Joy. Love.

Taryn stared, assessing the gift.

"You're not stuck." Vivian held onto the heart, presenting it to Taryn. "What happened last night doesn't have to be the whole of you. You can change, Taryn. You can choose better."

Silence pressed in, and Annie's heart swelled, willing her sister to believe.

Taryn's fingers trembled as she reached out and took the little heart, cradling it in her palm as though it might dissolve if she held it too hard. For the first time since the outburst, her lips parted into something that almost looked like a smile—shy, uneven, but real.

"Thank you," she whispered.

Vivian gave a nod, tossed her a wink, and slipped away.

Annie stepped closer, slipping her arm through her sister's, and Taryn didn't pull away. She just held the heart tighter, as though the stitched words were threads strong enough to bind her to something new. "It's beautiful," she whispered.

And in Annie's chest, hope blossomed—thin, but steady, like the first green shoots pushing through winter's frost.

The morning wore on with lessons and chores, but a hush seemed to trail after Annie and her twin. The other girls kept glancing at them, whispers trailing through the halls.

Taryn pulled the tiny heart from her pocket several times, her fingers brushing over the words again and again as if she were memorizing them by touch.

When lunch ended, Cassie seized Annie's hand in one of hers and Taryn's in the other. Her grip was firm and determined. "Come on, girls. No more of this sulking in corners. We're all in this together."

Before either twin could protest, Cassie tugged them to the edge of the room and called, "Circle, girls!"

The others hesitated but soon drew near. Gloria came first, again cuddling Mouser. But her face relaxed at the sight of Taryn holding Vivian's heart before slipping it into her pocket. Vivian joined as well, her confident smile urging the rest to follow. Soon the seven girls stood shoulder to shoulder, forming a ring with Annie and Taryn at its center.

Annie had longed for closeness, but she hadn't expected this. Could this, would this last?

As they stood together in silent unity, Sister Bernadette entered, her long habit swishing against the floor, and her wise observations taking in the scene. She paused, folding her hands, then spoke. "Ah, now, this is what I like to see. A circle of sisters, bound not by blood alone, but by grace. What good is a Christmas pageant if your hearts are divided?"

Her gaze swept over them, landing on Taryn. "Better to mend it all here and now, before you go out into the world."

Taryn stiffened beside Annie, then her sister's hand pressed harder into hers. Taryn lifted her chin, glancing around at each of the girls—at Gloria with Mouser, at Vivian with her encouraging smile, at Cassie's beaming grin. And Fiona, looking more like a mother than a girl, and Isabel, nodding elegantly, her glossy black braid tugging up and down.

"I was wrong," Taryn said at last. "And I don't want to stay this way."

The circle tightened, a ripple of relief and warmth moving through the girls. Mouser meowed from Gloria's arms, as if adding his own benediction.

Annie leaned closer to her twin, whispering so just she could hear: "See? We are not alone. We have sisters who care."

And for the first time in days, Taryn allowed herself a small, trembling smile.

CHAPTER 17

The morning's arithmetic class blurred with columns of figures that would not hold steady.

Numbers marched across Fiona's slate like soldiers lined for battle, each stroke of chalk sharp as bayonets. As she worked the sums, the nub of chalk gritted between her fingers. She kept her head bowed, hair pinned tight in its chignon, though a strand had slipped to tickle her cheek. But her hands itched, so she stopped to wipe them on her skirt.

Then, Fiona pressed the chalk too hard, snapping the end with a sharp crack. A murmur rippled through the room, and heat climbed her neck. "Goodness," she giggled, wiping her hands as though the chalk dust itself betrayed her.

Sister Catherine's head jerked up. "You think it's funny to misuse the chalk we graciously provide?" Forty-four years had left no softness in her face, and her dark glare pinned Fiona as nails through wood.

"Again, Fiona King. You are careless and clumsy—wicked like your mother."

A flush scalded Fiona's cheeks. The air in the room seemed to curdle. The other girls bent lower over their work. Her mother—always her mother, dragged into the open like a shameful banner. Fiona pressed her lips tight, her gaze smoldering against the floorboards.

"Sixteen years old," Sister Catherine said, her condescension swelling to fill the room, "the oldest among the girls here, and yet you still have not learned discipline. But how could you when you come from shame?"

Fiona's hands clenched around her chalk until her knuckles burned.

"Your mother," Sister Catherine went on, "was nothing but a poor Irish cook who brought a child into this world without a father to claim her. I know all the sordid details. She tried to keep you in secret, as though you were some shameful disease to be hidden away."

A gasp shivered through the room. Fiona's chest locked tight.

"Yes," Sister Catherine turned to the others, "so shame and ill-will flow through your veins."

Fiona's nails dug into her palms. She forced her face to remain still, though the hot sting behind her eyes threatened to betray her.

Sister Catherine turned back to her, close now. "Tell me, will you follow her path? Perhaps you've already begun. Poison in the pot, poison in the heart. Just like your mother."

Her words sliced deep, but she was not finished. "The Little Sisters have chosen you as cook." She leaned forward, her rancid breath bitter against Fiona's cheek. "A start to a career, perhaps. Unless, of course, you poison them too."

The classroom sat frozen, every girl pretending to study her numbers.

Sister Catherine straightened. "Hands."

Fiona obeyed, though her arms trembled.

The strap came down, burning lines across her palms. She bit her lip until the taste of iron filled her mouth.

Sister Catherine leaned closer, a whisper meant for Fiona alone. "You will learn humility, or you will learn pain. Perhaps both. Your mother managed neither." The words struck harder than the leather. Fiona's chin lifted, sharpening her expression with defiance. She would not bow to Sister Catherine or to anyone. Inside, a knot of fury coiled tighter, the kind that would never forgive and never forget.

The sting in her hands pulsed with each heartbeat, but worse was the fire in her chest. She could not endure under it or bear the silence of the classroom— all those bowed heads pretending not to hear what had been said.

Fiona turned abruptly. The sound of her boots drummed across the floorboards, making the other girls jump. For a moment, no one moved. Then she strode past Sister Catherine, chin lifted though her vision blurred, and flung open the door leading outside, a gust of cold and snow blowing into the room.

But she hesitated just a moment, looking back at her friends. Gasps rose from the girls, a few turning toward the door. Isabel pleaded, "Fiona will freeze if she goes outside!"

But Sister Catherine's arm came up, sharp as a blade. "Stop! No one goes after her." Her formidable glare raked the girls, daring them to disobey. "If she chooses rebellion, let her reap the consequences."

Fiona slammed the door shut, and the frozen day struck her like a wall—snow driving sideways, the blizzard shrieking against the stone walls of the school.

The wind stung her face raw and clawed at her hair, ripping strands loose from her chignon. Without a cloak or bonnet, she hurried into the snowstorm, her skirts whipping around her legs as she ran toward the shed.

The storm didn't subside for what seemed hours. Snow drummed against the shed where Fiona had taken shelter, but the wind's cry worked its way deep into her bones.

By the afternoon, the world lay buried in white, and she huddled in uneasy silence, glancing often at the door, hoping her friends would find her and the nun would not, until she fell asleep.

~ ~ ~

Gloria slipped away to find Fiona as soon as Sister Agnes dismissed her from her chores. Holding tight to her cloak, she pushed into the waning storm. She searched the yard and the outbuildings, her calls trembling against the wind.

Fiona lay in the shed, slumped against a stack of wood, skirts stiff with ice, skin blue-white, lips parted, and her breath shallow as a whisper.

"Oh, no!" Gloria gasped, dropping to her knees. "Fiona, can you hear me?"

A faint murmur slipped from Fiona's cracked lips, but there were no words—only a thread of life refusing to break.

Gloria pulled her close, wrapping her in her own cloak, and half dragged, half carried her back through the drifts. By the time she reached the orphanage steps, her arms ached and her voice was hoarse from calling.

The door burst open before her. Taryn was there, her jaw dropping as she saw Fiona limp in Gloria's arms.

Without hesitation, Taryn took charge. "Set her by the fire in the infirmary," Taryn commanded. A few girls scattered to help, fetching blankets, hot water, and anything she asked for.

Taryn knelt beside Fiona, her hands quick but gentle, stripping away the frozen garments, rubbing warmth back into rigid limbs, pressing cloths warmed by the hearth against her chilled skin. With tender words, she coaxed Fiona back. "Stay with me, now. Don't you dare leave us. You're safe. You're safe."

Fiona stirred, lashes fluttering against her cheeks. Her gold-flecked eyes opened a crack, unfocused. She shivered as warmth crept back into her veins but her pain became evident through her groans and whimpers.

~ ~ ~

Taryn sat at Fiona's bedside, the fire's glow catching on her pale, still face. The hours had blurred together—

wrapping her in wool, rubbing life into her stiff hands, spooning broth past lips that barely moved.

Each time Fiona stirred, Taryn's chest loosened. Each time she sank back into unconsciousness, fear tightened its grip again.

A voice broke through the hush. "You've done well, child."

Taryn, so focused on Fiona's care that the rest of the world had faded, looked up to see Sister Clare standing in the doorway, the lamplight tracing the kind lines of her face. Her presence was a balm—no harsh judgment, no iron rebuke like Sister Catherine's.

Sister Clare moved closer, carrying two steaming cups of herbal tea and set them down. She knelt beside Fiona, pressing a hand against her brow, then feeling along her wrist. After a long moment, she gave a small nod. "The fever is beginning to break. You kept her from slipping past the edge."

Relief surged through Taryn, though she tried not to let it show. "I—I just did what I could. Keeping her warm. Giving her broth. Holding her hand so she wouldn't drift away."

Sister Clare nodded. "And that is wisdom most learn through the years. Nursing is not just remedies and bandages. It is presence and patience, and you have a gift for it."

Taryn's chest swelled, then tightened. A gift. The word stirred something long buried beneath anger and shame.

Sister Clare pointed to the steaming cup on the bedside table. "Give her this tea when she can take it. It will soothe her lungs and warm her blood. And when she wakes, speak to her, and keep her anchored. You're doing more than you realize."

Taryn nodded, humbled. "It feels…like this is the only time I am at peace. When I'm serving and nursing someone." She paused and then pressed on. "Maybe I don't want to live with anger anymore. Maybe it's time to let it go."

Sister Clare smiled with approval. "Then you're choosing the better path. You've seen how bitterness and anger hurt others, and we'll not let such a thing happen again. Not to any of you. As we speak, Sister Catherine is being sequestered to office duties."

Taryn smiled. "Thank you for that, from all of us. I guess I must find a way to forgive and let go of the bitterness too."

Sister Clare gave her a nod. "And that is the best medicine of all."

Beside them, Fiona moaned and opened her eyes.

"I'm so pleased to see you awake, Fiona! Get well quickly." Sister Clare patted Fiona's shoulder, tucking the quilts tighter around her. "Fiona, God be with you. I'll leave you in Taryn's capable hands."

With that, she slipped out of the room, the door clicking behind her.

Now, in the hushed dark of night, a faint flush touched Fiona's cheeks where before there had been ashen gray. Taryn smoothed back a strand of damp auburn hair, her own heart trembling with relief.

"You almost slipped away," she took a sip of her tea, not certain Fiona could hear. "But I wouldn't let you."

A flicker stirred in Fiona's gaze, the brown deepened by flecks of gold. "Blathers, lass. Maybe you should have let me."

"No!" Taryn declared. "Don't say that, Fiona! I would never."

Silence filled the small room but for the crackle of fire. At last, Fiona turned her gaze toward her. "But maybe it would be easier if I weren't here. Perhaps Sister Catherine's right. I carry my mother's shame. It follows me like a shadow."

Taryn's heart ached at the rawness in her tone. She took Fiona's hand—still cool, though warmth was returning—and held it firm. "Then let's leave it all behind, you and me. Shame, guilt, anger—it'll drown us if we keep carrying it. I've been clinging to my own bitterness, you know. About the almshouse. About being cast off as though I was worth nothing. I thought it made me strong, but it's made me hollow."

She pressed on, her words like a vow. "When I care for someone—when I fight for their breath to return, for their heart to keep beating—that's when I feel peace. That's who I want to be, Fiona. Not the angry girl the world tried to make me."

Fiona's eyes glistened, though no tears fell. Her lips trembled before she spoke. "Aye, then maybe I can learn to lay mine down, too, if I can figure out how. The shame and guilt. I've been carrying them as though they were stitched to my skin."

"They aren't yours. They never were."

A bond formed in that hush—something deeper than friendship, forged not from duty or chance, but from the choice to hold one another's brokenness without judgment.

"Then let's leave it behind." Fiona brushed a tear away. "Together."

And for the first time, Taryn allowed herself a small smile, tender and true. "Together."

Taryn clasped Fiona's hand, feeling the warmth returning. Their gaze met, and in that look, a vow bound them—no longer two girls defined by what had been taken from them, but two souls choosing what they might give.

CHAPTER 18

The following evening, the girls assembled together, waiting for the fourth advent candle to come to life. A draft in the chapel tugged at Taryn's sleeves as she stood beside her sister before the Advent wreath table. They had been given the task of lighting the love candle together.

She was ready to move on, but she wasn't quite ready for something so…collaborative.

Annie reached for the candle, but Taryn moved in first, steady and decisive, slipping into comfortable control before her sister could. The match hissed to life in Taryn's hand, and she lit the love candle.

Taryn drew in a breath, words spilling out, as they always did when she was holding onto the lead and fighting for control. "Hope, joy, and peace— these must not be thought of as mere ornaments or luxuries. I think they must be part of love itself. But love…" She paused, teeth catching her bottom lip before she let the last words dangle in the cold air. "Love is often elusive and hard to find, hidden behind doubt, sorrow, pain, or silence."

Beside her, Annie's eyes flashed surprise, then she tipped her chin upward as though searching the rafters for wisdom.

"Or maybe," Annie said with a bright smile, "hope, joy, and peace are the signs that love is already here. All four can bring life and meaning to our world. They can heal us, if we let them. But often, we forget to embrace them—or we push them away." Her hazelgreen gaze darted toward Taryn, almost as if the words were offered as a truce—or another scolding.

Taryn's fists clenched at her sides. "It isn't as simple as that," she muttered, a low press of steel beneath her words.

Annie shifted, fussing with the sleeve of her dress. "You always think it isn't simple. You make everything difficult."

"Because everything is difficult. Someone has to be realistic and state the truth." Taryn's tone sharpened before she could rein it back. The flame on the fourth candle trembled in the draft, as though mirroring her emotions.

"You mean your truth!" Annie shot back, harsh and angry. "It always has to be your way and your truth. You don't need to control everything. We were supposed to light the candle together, Taryn!"

A murmur stirred through the group, and Sister Rose cut through the tension. "That will be enough, girls."

Sister Rose guided Annie aside, but the slump of her shoulders and her quivering lips brought Taryn a prick of shame. Annie turned every problem into a simple solution, but how often she left the harder parts unspoken.

Taryn remained by the candles, her spine stiff and her fists unclenching only when she realized she had dug crescent moons into her palms.

The candle burned on, fragile but steady. Taryn stared at it, her jaw tight. Hope, joy, peace, and love— those words rang warm when Annie spoke them. But when she did, they always seemed to taste bitter and empty.

Sister Rose took a few steps forward before addressing the group. "I had a sister once. She was bright as morning light and stubborn as an ox. We quarreled more times than I can count. And one day…she just left, angry and hurt. I thought I'd lost her forever."

Taryn leaned forward, her frown deepening. "Did she come back?"

A wistful smile tugged at Sister Rose's lips as she grasped Taryn's hand. "Not for many years. But when she did, it wasn't because I controlled her or demanded she change. It was because she knew— despite all the wrong between us—that I still loved her. That door of sister love was never shut."

Taryn's heart pricked. She'd spoken so many sharp words, built so many walls in her own spirit. Forgiving didn't feel easy. And changing? That seemed like a mountain far too steep.

Sister Rose motioned for Annie to join them. When she did, Sister Rose took both of their hands but addressed the group. "Love can cover a multitude of hurt and offense, dear ones. Not by pretending the pain isn't real, but by choosing to love in spite of it. Forgiving and changing are not lightning strikes. They are often long, slow steps. Sometimes halting, sometimes clumsy—but a way of moving forward all the same."

Taryn swallowed hard. "So…I don't have to be perfect all at once?"

"No, child," Sister Rose smiled tenderly. "The Lord delights in the journey, not just the destination."

She turned back to the group. "And this is for all of you, not just Taryn and Annie."

A small smile broke across Taryn's face. The burden on her chest didn't vanish, but it felt lighter somehow. Maybe forgiveness wasn't a cliff to leap from. Maybe it was a road she could walk.

Annie glanced at Taryn and then addressed everyone, prim and proper in posture, though her words tumbled out with impulsive eagerness. "I think sometimes we think forgiveness is like washing a dress. One scrub, and it's spotless. But it might be more like mending a tear. You stitch and stitch, and it takes patience. And sometimes, you prick your finger along the way."

Taryn blinked, surprised at her twin's depth.

Annie continued. "But in the end, the dress can still be worn, and maybe it's even stronger where it was torn."

The room grew still. Taryn's throat tightened, emotion welling in her chest. "That's… beautiful, Willow."

Annie's cheeks flushed pink. "Thank you. I'm just saying what came to mind."

Sister Rose chuckled and let go of the girls hands. "And you said it well, my dear. Sometimes the simplest words carry the deepest truths."

Taryn reached out, grasping Annie's slender hands in her own and forming a tiny, private sister circle. "Maybe, someday, I can mend things with you? I want to, you know. I really do."

Annie swallowed, tears spilling onto her cheeks. "I never expect you to be perfect, Taryn. Just to keep on trying."

Taryn nodded, and for the first time in a long while, she didn't feel quite so alone on the path toward forgiveness. Between Sister Rose's steady wisdom and Annie's tender heart, hope stirred.

Sister Rose addressed Sister Agnes at the back of the chapel. "Why don't you oversee an impromptu Christmas play practice with the girls? We can have the little ones join them tomorrow."

Sister Agnes nodded. "A fine idea. Vivian, take the lead, please."

The girls murmured their thank you as Sister Rose left them to practice.

"All right, girls. Places!" Vivian waved an arm as she motioned the girls into position. "Let's get on with it. Mary—Izzy, that's you—front and center. Spine straight and chin high like the holy mother herself."

Isabel glided forward with practiced grace, her long black braid swinging down her back. She tapped her lip, then folded her hands. "Aye, like this, Viv?"

"Perfect," Vivian declared. "Joseph, you'll stand beside her…oh, wait. I'm playing him." The girls giggled.

Gloria, her round face glowing, raised her hand as she so often did. "Do I sing all the verses of the carol or just the first?"

"All of them, Little Lark." Vivian tossed her a grin. "Your song is the star over Bethlehem."

Gloria blushed, her golden pigtails brushing her shoulders as she ducked her head.

In the corner, Annie bit her lip as she adjusted her skirts. "Maybe I should just stay in the back. I seem to keep bumping into everyone."

But Fiona was already at her side. "Nae, Annie. You belong right up front. Angel Gabriel doesn't hide in corners."

"Yes," Vivian added. "If anyone's meant to announce glad tidings, it's you. Don't argue." Annie licked her lips and nodded.

Taryn stood a little apart, her shawl folded over her arm. The girls seemed to have forgotten her embarrassing argument with Annie, and she was glad of it. Maybe everything will work out after all.

Cassie strode over, her ledger tucked beneath her arm. She pushed her spectacles up her nose. "You're the head wise man, Taryn, and I'm head shepherd. We need you."

"I don't like pretending," Taryn muttered.

Cassie sniffed. "This is not pretending—it's an important historical reenactment. And you'll be excellent."

Taryn bit her lip to hold back a retort—and a smile. The rehearsal stumbled forward—lines forgotten, places missed, Vivian cracking jokes at every turn. Yet whenever Isabel faltered, Gloria's encouragement steadied her. Whenever Annie shrank, Fiona lifted her up. And when Taryn grew rigid, Cassie reassured her. By the end, laughter rang out as brightly as Gloria's carol, and the circle of girls seemed to be whole again.

Taryn sucked in a steadying breath. She and her twin were not on the edge of things—they were at the heart of it.

Just then, the door creaked open. Sister Rose entered, her gaze sweeping the scene with a knowing gentleness. "My girls, I'm pleased to hear your good cheer. But before we call it a night, I must speak to you about Sister Catherine. Come and join me on the front pew, please."

Once they settled, Sister Rose began. "Young ladies, I want to tell you something that may help you understand why Sister Catherine has been the way she is."

Taryn sighed as the girls exchanged glances, some skeptical, others curious. Gloria scooped up Mouser and wrapped her arms around him.

Sister Rose's gaze swept over them, lingering on Taryn and then on Fiona for a heartbeat before she continued. "You all know how harsh she can be, how strict her rules feel. And many of you have felt wounded by them. But did you know that Sister Catherine herself carries a deep wound?"

"She once had a younger brother, and she loved him. But there came a time when that child needed her, and Catherine could not protect him. The pain of that failure cut deep. So deep, she began to believe that safety could only be found in strict rules that never bend or falter. So, she built her life upon them."

Silence fell over the room, and Taryn's breath caught. The sting of recognition shot through her— how she had hurt Mouser out of her own tangled pain and the way Catherine's hurt had shaped her hardness.

Sister Rose frowned. "Sister Catherine has expressed remorse, but you will no longer be left in her care. What she's done is wrong. Terribly wrong. But her coldness, her sharpness—these are the masks she wears to cover her brokenness."

Isabel whispered, "So…she's broken, like us?"

Sister rose sighed. "Yes. Very much so. Which is why I ask you to see her not just as a stern mistress, but as a soul in need of grace. Forgive her, even if she does not ask. For soon…” She drew in a long breath. “Soon, after the New Year, she will be leaving the Irish Rose.” Gasps circled the group.

“Her path will take her to a place with no children. And though it may bring you relief, I hope it also brings compassion. For even in her leaving, Catherine’s wound remains. And perhaps, in your hearts, love can begin to stitch where life has torn.”

The fire cracked, casting wavering light across the girls’ faces. Taryn sat very still, her chest tight but her spirit lighter. Sister Catherine had hurt them—but behind her icy exterior was a heart that had once loved and lost.

For the first time, Taryn felt more sorrow than bitterness toward the woman.

CHAPTER 19

The chapel brimmed with warmth and anticipation. Candle flames danced against stained-glass windows, their glow casting streaks of crimson and gold onto the worn wooden pews. Neighbors, benefactors, and curious onlookers packed every row, their shoulders brushing, and their breath misting in the cool Christmas Eve air.

Isabel recognized Mrs. Callahan from the bakery, Father Dunne, and a cluster of parish women with kerchiefs tied tight against the chapel's chill. Many were unfamiliar faces. Yet all eyes seemed to hold the same expectation—that the girls of the Irish Rose Orphan Asylum would deliver a Christmas Eve performance that stirred hearts and reminded them of the holy night in Bethlehem.

Isabel sighed. Why did they choose her to play Mary, the mother of God? Gracious!

The other girls bustled around her in the corner near the stage, each costume a bit crooked despite Isabel's earlier adjustments. Vivian's red hair stuck out from her head cloth in an unruly tuft. Isabel reached up and smoothed it without a word, but Vivian winked in reply, her bright cheerfulness masking something Isabel had learned to recognize as fear.

"Do you think they'll clap?" Vivian whispered.

"Aye, of course, Joseph." Isabel could not abide hesitation, not tonight. "Now hold still."

Cassie gathered the younger ones into a circle, whispering last reminders with the air of a little teacher, as though she alone could keep the group from toppling into chaos. Some would be sheep, some shepherds like herself, and a few as cows, donkeys, and a dog.

A flicker of thankfulness swelled in Isabel's heart for Cassie's motherly control of the wee ones.

In the far corner, Annie and Taryn stood side by side, their identical features tense. Annie as Gabriel and Taryn as a wise man, her jaw set a little too tight. If they ruined this with their rift, she would....

She stopped herself, pressing her braid between her fingers. No. Tonight had to be different.

Gloria bit a fingernail, her nervousness evident to all. Isabel stepped forward and stilled her little sister's trembling hands. "Breathe," she said, though her tone held the weight of command. "You'll do fine, my Little Lark."

Gloria nodded, though her lips quivered. And then—music. The organ began its low, solemn prelude.

Isabel's spine straightened, every nerve alert. From her place in the wing, Sister Rose's gaze caught hers, a steady flame behind her kind countenance, and the faintest nod passed between them. It was enough.

Light spilled across the small stage, catching the edges of a wooden crèche, straw scattered across the floor. One by one, the girls stepped out. Isabel walked with measured grace, her chin high, her movements precise, as though she alone bore the duty of carrying them through. A perfect Mary.

The audience hushed.

Annie and Taryn entered together but tension still floated between them. The twin's fracture seemed to be one step forward and two steps back. Yet when their song rose in harmony for the angel's hymn, Isabel's heart tightened. Perhaps music could bind what words could not.

Playing Joseph, Vivian almost tripped over her staff, but recovered with a radiant smile so charming, a few patrons chuckled. Isabel pressed her lips together and said nothing. Better a stumble masked with joy than one that shattered the moment.

Cassie gave the Scripture reading, her chin tilted and every syllable measured, as though she had rehearsed in secret. The audience leaned in, rapt.

And then Gloria, small and trembling, stepped forward with her solo. Isabel's breath caught. Her voice quivered at first, then steadied, blooming into something pure, tender, and beautiful. Isabel's eyes stung, though she would never admit to tears.

When the final carol swelled, Isabel sang with all the control and strength she possessed, her voice blending with the others, lifting praise to the heavens. Her Irish Rose sisters—divided, wounded, and uncertain—became for one fragile moment a single sound, a single light, a single family.

The last note faded, and silence hovered. Then—applause, rich and exuberant, filling every corner of the chapel.

Isabel exhaled at last, though her posture never faltered. The girls collapsed into whispers, giggles, and relieved sighs. Vivian clutched Isabel's arm, almost bouncing. "Did you see? They loved us!"

"Aye," Isabel said, smoothing her braid. Inside, though, her heart was pounding with a fierceness she could not tame.

Gloria wept, and Cassie wrapped an arm around her shoulders. Annie and Taryn stood together, smiling. Isabel looked at them all—her forever sisters. Soon they would scatter, sent into service among strangers, each to her own uncertain fate.

But tonight, under candlelight and applause, they had been whole. And that wholeness was a gift she would etch into memory with all the precision of her finest penmanship—never to be forgotten.

~ ~ ~

An hour later, the dormitory was dim, warmed by the glow of a small fire crackling in the grate. The air carried the mingled scents of pine boughs—gathered earlier from the courtyard—and the faintest trace of beeswax from the chapel candles still clinging to their dresses.

The girls had changed into their nightclothes, and a few of the smaller ones had begged to join them, too excited to sleep. The pageant had left them stirred from within.

They sprawled across narrow beds and braided rugs, giggles tumbling over one another in bursts of laughter and sighs. Vivian, always the first to bubble over, leaned back against her pillow, her grin shining.

"Did you hear them clap? I thought the roof might shake loose!"

Cassie smiled, her hands folded in her lap. "It wasn't only the clapping. They were listening. Truly listening. Even the little children sat still."

Gloria hugged her knees to her chest, her face still flushed from her solo. "I thought my voice would fail me. But when I opened my mouth…" Her words broke into a breathless laugh. "It was as if something carried me."

"Nae. Not something," Isabel tapped a finger to her lip reaching for the right words. "Someone. I felt Him with us. From the very first note."

The room hushed at that, the younger girls turning toward her with awe-struck smiles. Isabel seldom spoke of feelings. Her words were measured, careful, and precise. Yet tonight, she could not hold them back.

"When Gloria sang, it was as though heaven leaned nearer. And when we all joined at the end…" She drew a breath, pressing her fingers to the edge of her braid. "I knew we were not singing alone."

For a moment, silence lingered, heavy with meaning. Then Fiona, calm and thoughtful, nodded. "Aye. I felt it too. As if the Christ Child Himself were among us."

Vivian's grin became a gentler smile. "Maybe that's why the audience grew silent. They felt it, even if they didn't know."

Cassie clasped her hands tighter, her gaze shining. "Sister Rose always says the story of Bethlehem is meant to live again in us. Perhaps it did tonight."

Annie and Taryn exchanged a glance. Annie murmured first, just above a whisper. "For once, it felt like…all the sharp things were gone. Just for a little while."

Taryn nodded, a sigh escaping her lips. "Like peace."

Gloria buried her face against her knees and gave a muted sob—not of sorrow, but of awe. "Aye, then maybe that's what it means, what Sister Rose keeps saying. Emmanuel. God with us."

The fire popped, and the sound drew Isabel's attention back to the flames. She let the others' words settle deep inside her, engraving the moment into memory.

Because soon the world would scatter them. But tonight, here in the Irish Rose dormitory, the memory carried the echo of Bethlehem itself. And Isabel, who always noticed everything, felt certain that God had indeed been among them.

As the fire burned low, the little ones were shooed off to bed, while the older girls remained near the hearth. Their earlier laughter and chatter faded into drowsy wonder. Isabel leaned against the arm of the chair near the hearth, her hands folded in her lap, tapping her fingers on her nightgown. She wanted to burn the evening in her mind's eye, like ink pressed onto parchment.

A creak broke the silence. The door opened, and Sister Rose stepped inside, her dark habit shadowed by the candle she carried. The girls straightened, though their eyes still glowed with the warmth of the evening. "I thought I might find you all still awake. The evening's light lingers, does it not?"

Vivian beamed. "They clapped, Sister. Loud as thunder!"

"And Gloria sang like an angel," Cassie added, squeezing Gloria's hand.

Gloria hid her face, but Sister Rose beamed. "I heard it, and I heard more. You gave them not only a pageant, my girls—you gave them Bethlehem, alive and breathing."

A hush fell. Isabel lifted her chin, the words striking deep. She wanted to capture them, to etch them across her memory.

Bethlehem, alive and breathing. Yes. That was what she had felt.

Sister Rose moved closer to the fire, setting the candle on the mantel. The light caught her face, lined with years yet bright with something eternal. "You will carry this night with you, I pray. For soon…" She paused, her gaze sweeping across them all. "Soon you will go forth into homes not your own, into duties that will test you. But remember this— that Emmanuel, God with us, was with you tonight, and He will be with you still."

Annie and Taryn, seated side by side though silent, exchanged another quick glance. Taryn's hand shifted toward her sister's.

Vivian whispered, almost to herself, "Then we won't ever be alone."

"No," Sister Rose said firmly. "Never alone."

From the folds of her habit, she drew a small pouch and held it close, not opening it yet. "In time, I have a parting gift for each of you. A token to remind you of who you are, and of the bond that cannot be broken." Her fingers brushed the pouch as though it carried something fragile, precious.

"But not tonight. Tonight is for rest and for joy."

The girls leaned forward with curiosity, but Sister Rose smiled. "Patience. The Lord Himself waited until the fullness of time. You can wait a few days more." A ripple of laughter passed through the dormitory. Isabel allowed herself a rare, small smile, though she kept her posture as straight as ever.

A gift. She longed to know what it was.

CHAPTER 20

Fiona rose before dawn, the way she always did, and tied her apron at her waist. When she entered the kitchen, the scent of rising bread rising slow and steady in the heat of the hearth, filled the room. Sister Bernadette stood at a great pot, her sleeves rolled up, humming a hymn as she stirred porridge. This morning, she had sprinkled in cinnamon, a small extravagance for Christmas Day.

"Happy Christmas, Fiona," Sister Bernadette said, her voice warm and kind. "You've been a joy and a blessing to work with these past few years, and I will miss you terribly."

Fiona froze a moment, her attention flicking up at the novice nun. Miss her? The words caught her off guard. She turned back to her work, sliding the dough into the oven. Wiping her hands on her apron, she murmured, "Happy Christmas, Sister. Thank you. I've learned much under your instructions."

"I think you are ready for your new position and capable of running a kitchen on your own. Don't doubt your abilities, Fiona, and leave the shadows of the past behind."

Fiona nodded, ready to thank her again, but the fire shifted, sending sparks scattering across the hearthstones. She muttered under her breath and grabbed the poker, pushing the logs back into place. Her movements were brisk, controlled—better to focus on the task at hand than on the knot of feeling tightening in her chest.

She never let on how tired or unsure she was.

But it was Christmas, a day to celebrate the birth of Christ, a day to let in joy for a few hours. She straightened, brushing a flour smudge from her cheek.

She turned to her superior. "Thank you for that, Sister."

From the upstairs dormitories, the faint creak of floorboards and muffled whispers drifted down. Soon the girls would come, bright-eyed in their Sunday best, eager for surprises Sister Bernadette had gathered. Fiona had helped her wrap them in butcher paper days before, and keeping the gifts a secret had been no easy task.

Fiona smiled at the thought of their delight— new mittens, a warm hat, and a peppermint stick each. Simple things, but treasures in this house. Sister Bernadette would hand them out and asked Fiona to help—to make sure each child's eyes lit with that spark of wonder. That was her gift to them. Not laughter— Fiona had little of that to spare—but care, protection, and faithfulness.

The smell of cinnamon rose with the steam of the porridge, wrapping the room in warmth. Sister Bernadette hummed a Christmas hymn, and the melody stirred something deep inside Fiona, something she pressed down. She swiped at her chignon, tucked an errant strand behind her ear, and swallowed her emotions.

It was Christmas morning, and no matter what rested on her heart, she would make it bright for the others. That she would!

Thanks to last night's patrons, they had enough small oranges for each girl to share with one other. Better yet, one kind couple donated a large bowl of plum pudding for tonight's Christmas dinner, and each girl would get a generous spoonful to enjoy. What a feast!

The sleepy girls gathered, still rubbing their eyes, their chatter bright against the cold of Christmas morning. Fiona handed each their Christmas gift, and their laughter rang through the hall as they tugged the hats and gloves on, showing each other, comparing colors, and tasting the peppermint with sticky grins, even before breakfast.

Something they could only do on Christmas morning. Fiona stood apart, arms folded, her apron still dusted with flour. She watched them, her heart pinched tight. This was the part she never knew how to join—the giggles and the innocent delight. She loved each one of them, but always from a distance, like someone guarding the doorway against a world she didn't trust.

Sister Bernadette touched her arm. "Fiona, come and enjoy a peppermint stick."

Fiona shook her head. "Aye, but I must mind the bread before it burns."

Yet she was caught off guard as one of the little ones wrapped her mittened hands around Fiona's waist in a quick hug before handing her a peppermint stick and darting off again.

"Oh, my goodness," Fiona whispered.

For the briefest moment, as snowflakes drifted past the frosted windows and the girls twirled in their new hats, she almost smiled. But the world still sat heavy on her shoulders, and she would not let it slip.

After breakfast, Fiona joined everyone as they gathered in the chapel where garlands of evergreen brightened the stone walls and candles flickered like small stars. They expressed their joy in carols—some strong and sure, others shy and wavering. The Christmas story was read with such tenderness that even the youngest sat still as though the angel's message had just reached them fresh from heaven. Awe hushed the room, the joy of the morning clinging to them like the warmth of a quilt.

Fiona sat near the back, her hands folded in her lap, her gaze steady on the nativity scene at the altar. The carved wooden figures, simple and worn, seemed almost alive in the glow of the candles. How did the Little Sisters of St. Joseph, where she'd soon become cook, celebrate the holy day in their orphanage? Was their chapel filled with the same sweetness? Did they have peppermint sticks to pass to children, or did they keep their joy reserved and cloistered?

In a little while, she would be finding her way among strangers. No longer the "Mother" to the girls here, but the head cook in the sisters' kitchen. How many mouths would she be stirring pots for then? Twenty? Fifty? More? She'd never been told. Would she be able to keep up?

Her throat tightened. She told herself it was not fear—she had no use for fear—but something else. Her future loomed wide and uncertain, yet every step forward seemed to pull her farther from the only home she had ever kept, here at Irish Rose. She glanced around the room as these sweet little ones would still laugh and squabble, still call for someone to tie their ribbons or chase away the dark dreams of the night—but it would not be her.

She drew a sharp breath, steadying her shoulders. She could not falter, not now. Christ had come into the world, born in a manger, a stranger to this world as she was to hers.

But He saw her too. Still, her heart whispered questions she dared not speak—What if I fail—like my mother? What if I am not enough? How do I let go of these rotten thoughts once and for all? She whispered, "God, help me, please."

The last carol faded, the final "Amen" rose in a joyful chorus, and the girls scattered in a flutter of skirts and laughter, their joy carrying them into the day. Fiona lingered a moment longer in the wooden pew, her gaze on the flickering Christ candle, as though its steady flame might hold an answer for her.

Sister Bernadette touched Fiona's arm as she passed. "I've got lunch in hand. You go outside with the rest of the girls and play in the snow. It's not a suggestion. Go and have fun, Fiona."

Fiona blinked, startled as if the sister had spoken in some strange tongue. Play? She had not thought of such a thing for herself in a long while. Still, Sister Bernadette's tone left no room for a protest. Fiona gave a sharp little nod, wiping her hands on her skirts—a habit she'd acquired in the Irish Rose kitchens.

The girls were already tumbling through the back doors into the yard, their shouts and laughter rising like bells in the crisp air. The older ones guided the smaller, tugging hats snug, pulling mittens straight, and watching so no one slipped on the icy steps. Fiona followed, reluctant but unwilling to defy Sister Bernadette.

The yard lay blanketed in white, sparkling in the pale December sun. Isabel and Gloria flopped side by side into the snow, swinging arms and legs to shape sister angels together. Their giggles rang out as the powder clung to their coats and lashes. Across the way, Annie and Taryn did the same, their mittened hands brushing as they worked, leaving a pair of angels joined at the wings.

The little ones shrieked with delight as the older girls pulled some of them on makeshift sleds— old boards tied with rope—and others tumbled down the small hill by the fence. Snowballs flew in clumsy arcs, more laughter than aim, the game spilling across the yard with reckless joy.

Fiona stood near the doorway at first, her arms folded tight across her chest. She told herself she was watching over them, making sure no one caught a chill or ran too far. But the truth pressed at her ribs—she was afraid to step into their world of play, afraid she might break something fragile in herself.

Yet when one of the smallest girls tugged at her sleeve, holding out two red mittens full of snowball that failed to form, Fiona couldn't help the low chuckle that escaped her. She crouched, formed a ball and handed it to her. "There you go, wee one." The child beamed, then darted back into the fray.

For a fleeting moment, as the loveliness of laughter swirled around her, Fiona let herself take it in— the freedom and sheer joy of it. And though she did not lie down to make a snow angel herself, she stood a little looser, a little lighter, watching the girls enjoy the world around them.

~ ~ ~

By dinnertime, the dining hall glowed warm with candlelight, the long tables crowded with steaming dishes—roasted chicken, whipped potatoes, creamed corn, and the golden loaves Fiona had tended to that morning.

The girls sat in their rows, cheeks flushed from play, their hats and mittens still drying by the hearth. A happy hum filled the room, laughter bubbling as freely as the gravy poured over plates.

Fiona moved among them, serving here, steadying a cup there, her sharp eyes making sure each plate was filled and each child content.

Then, in the middle of the merriment, a sudden scuffle stirred beneath the table. A streak of black darted between the girls' boots—Mouser. He sprang up onto a bench with a twitch of his tail, and in his mouth wriggled a limp gray mouse.

Gasps filled the room, followed by squeals and peals of laughter. The girls leaned back, half horrified, half delighted. Mouser strutted with pride, dropping the unfortunate creature at the feet of Gloria as if bestowing a treasure.

"Oh, my goodness!" Fiona rushed forward, her apron already in hand. But before she could sweep the rodent away, the girls dissolved into fits of giggles, clapping their hands.

"Look, he's adding to our Christmas dinner! It's his Christmas gift to us," Gloria said, her laughter infectious.

Even Sister Bernadette chuckled, though she shook her head. "Mouser, you rascal." She bent to shoo the mouse away.

The tomcat sat back on his haunches, tail flicking, as though waiting for thanks.

The whole hall rang with laughter, their mirth spilling over until Fiona's lips twitched in spite of her stern resolve.

She bit into her tiny portion of plum pudding, savoring the treat, and for once, even she could not hold back the joy of the day.

CHAPTER 21

Annie couldn't believe Taryn had lost her Irish Rose locket. She had decided to wear it to celebrate New Year's Eve, but now it was gone. How could that happen? Surely, no one took it.

"Taryn's locket must be here somewhere." She scanned the dormitory. "If we search together, it will turn up."

But instead of harmony, a low tide of mutters rose around her.

"She ought to take better care of it," Cassie mumbled.

"It wouldn't be lost at all if she'd wear it instead of tucking it away," Isabel added, sharp as a needle prick.

"She was planning to!" Annie defended, the taste of unease bitter. She longed to smooth the air with a light jest, but even she knew laughter would shatter against the divisive weight in the room.

Taryn's fists curled tight, and her jaw looked hard enough to splinter the wooden beams above.

The quarrel swelled—bickering and little barbs flung like gravel. Annie's nerves pulled thin, a fragile thread straining to keep from breaking. She'd vowed to support her sister, no matter what.

And then, silence.

Sister Rose stood in the doorway assessing them with a piercing glare. She pressed a hand to her own heart, then lifted that hand and pointed—slowly, deliberately—to each of them. Disappointment lingered in her gaze before she turned and slipped away without a word.

The hush she left behind was sharper than any scolding, and Annie's cheeks burned with shame.

She offered a silent prayer, then, she caught a glint of light from the chain as it lay against the side of the cupboard. She almost squealed as she scooped it up.

"I found it!" The chain coiled like a sleeping thing in her hand, the locket glinting in the dim light. Relief swelled through her, tender and aching.

"Here," she whispered, pressing the locket into Taryn's palm. Annie's fingers lingered on the locket in Taryn's hand, reluctant to let go of the fragile peace.

Her sister blinked, and Annie saw the smallest easing in her shoulders, the faintest crack in her armor. For a moment, the room remained still. Then, around them, murmurs of apology rose—halting and awkward, but real.

Cassie shifted, her hands trembling. "I shouldn't have said what I did. It wasn't kind, and I'm sorry, Taryn."

Another followed, words spilling fast as if to cover the silence. Fiona this time. "Blathers, lassies! We've no business turning against each other. Not when we'll soon part, and not when our sisterly love is what we'll miss most."

One by one, they spoke—words weaving into love. They vowed to set aside such nonsense, to guard one another instead of wound, and to let no petty quarrel dim the little time they had left together. As they spoke, they drew nearer to Taryn—hesitant hands brushing her arm or her shoulder, a shy touch of comfort. Their circle tightened until she stood at the center, surrounded not by judgment but by care.

In that moment, something changed. Taryn's jaw loosened and her fists unfurled. Her dark hazel eyes glistened as though some unseen tide had reached the shore. She said nothing, but she didn't have to.

Annie saw it—the astonishment of a girl unaccustomed to being loved, chosen, and cared for despite her walls. And in that silence, Annie grabbed onto the hope that the year ahead may hold a promise of peace.

"May I?" She motioned to put the locket on her sister, and Taryn nodded. As she did, a sweet, new connection formed.

Perhaps it wasn't just a locket they had found. Perhaps it was a chain of trust that would bind them through time and space.

"If we are to scatter, let us not leave empty-handed," Isabel said. "Let us tuck prayers and Scriptures into each other's carpetbags, so that when the days feel long and lonely, we will find one another's words waiting."

The suggestion caught in Annie's heart like a puff of wind filling a sail. One by one, the girls nodded. Cassie disappeared to gather ink and paper, receiving Sister Rose's enthusiastic blessing, of course.

Within minutes, Annie grinned as quills scratched into the hush as each girl wrote tiny, heartfelt letters to her Irish Rose sisters—a verse remembered, a prayer offered, or a blessing shaped by her sisters' own hand.

Annie bent low over her page, pausing now and then to search for the right words. She licked her lips, thoughtful, and let her heart pour out a simple prayer—that Taryn may know she was never alone, not even when she believed herself so.

When the writing was finished, they stole to the row of old empty carpetbags—donated, with fabric frayed by years of use. Into each one, they slipped their folded offerings, secrets of love and faith waiting to be read. Annie slid hers into Taryn's bag with trembling care, vowing to stay close, no matter what.

"Aye, we will stay in touch." Isabel's words grew roots in the silence, taken up by each girl in turn.

"We must stay in touch," they echoed, weaving promises together like threads on a loom.

Warmth unfurled in Annie's chest. For all the partings ahead, for all the unknown miles that would stretch between them, there was this—a covenant of prayer and love. A covenant strong enough, perhaps, to bind them even when distance or years tried to tear them apart. And though Taryn said nothing, her sister's hand brushed the locket at her throat, then hovered there.

A hush lingered after the last promise was spoken, a fragile hope filled with the unspoken ache of parting. Annie's gaze lifted upward, as it often did when she longed for ideas larger than herself, and then she felt a spark—a thought, half formed but full of hope.

"We could write, not just once, but continually," she proposed before the full idea tumbled free. "A letter that travels from one to another, round and round. A Round Robin, they call it. Each of us adds her piece, her news, her prayer, and then passes it on. When it comes back to you, it carries everyone's stories with it. It's like sitting together again, even when we're scattered to the four winds."

For a moment, silence met her words—then it cracked, warm and sudden, into exclamations of delight.

"That's just like you, Annie." Vivian brushed at her cheeks with the corner of her sleeve. "Forever thinking of ways to stitch us together like patchwork."

Cassie clasped Annie's hand. "I would treasure such a thing. To hear you all, one by one…it would feel like coming home."

The spark grew brighter, urging Annie to say more. "I heard of it from my adoptive mother. She and her four sisters passed a Round Robin between them all their lives. The letter never ended—it circled and circled, like the seasons. They carried each other that way, even when they could not be together. It only stopped when she died."

The girls leaned closer, listening as though her words were candlelight in a darkened room. But Taryn's eyes flickered in a way Annie knew too well. A sharp glint—jealousy, quick and fierce—flashed at the mention of Annie's adoptive mother, the family she had known while Taryn had gone without. Taryn's lips pressed thin, fists curling at her sides.

Annie's heart squeezed. She reached for her sister's hand. "Oh, Taryn—I'm sorry. I shouldn't have."

But Taryn shook her head. "It's all right." She hesitated, then added, "You loved her. You were meant to love her. And I—" Something seemed to catch in her throat, but she pressed on with quiet strength. "I'll still write. I'll still be part of it."

Warmth filled Annie's heart. She gave Taryn's hand a little squeeze, as though to seal the fragile truce between them.

Around them, the other girls smiled through their tears. Isabel spoke again, bright with conviction. "Then it's decided. A crackin' Round Robin for us all. A letter that never ends."

Tears welled, unashamed now, slipping down cheeks and caught by careful fingers. Even Taryn let out a sigh that seemed to ease something long held.

Annie imagined their scribbled notes crossing miles, carrying bits of ribbon or pressed flowers tucked inside, a chain of love winding on forever. Her laugh tangled with the tears, until the two could not be separated.

In the silence that followed, a new strength emerged—silent but sure. A strength that rose not from any single heart, but from all of them bound together with threads woven into something lasting.

Annie pressed her hand to her chest, and for the first time, she felt the leaving would not mean losing. It would mean carrying each other into the wide world— and being carried in return.

As the others drifted off to their cots, Annie shuffled to hers, her fingers clumsy with the hooks of her dress. She was always scattered at the end of a long day.

Beside her, Taryn's motions were brisk and exact—her braid unwound with practiced speed, her nightdress slipped on neat and smooth. The contrast between them was almost comical—Annie fumbling with stockings she'd left in a ball, and Taryn folding each garment as if order itself depended upon her.

Annie glanced at her sister and let out a small laugh. "You'd think, after all this time, I'd have learned to keep myself a bit tidier."

Taryn smirked, the edge of her mouth twitching. "You've learned plenty. Just not that."

The teasing was gentle, but it eased something in Annie's chest. She sat on the edge of the bed, pulling her braids over her shoulders. "We've come so far, haven't we? From those first days when I couldn't even fold a sheet without Sister Agnes sighing." She smiled. "And you—so quiet, so locked away. I thought I'd never hear you laugh."

Taryn paused in brushing out her braid, the candlelight catching her eyes. For a moment, the wall in her expression thinned. "And yet you did. We both changed."

Annie swallowed, her agreement reverent. "Yes, and we've still so far to go. So much we don't yet know of the world or of ourselves, and it frightens me sometimes. But it also feels…hopeful. Like stepping into a story still being written.”

For once, Taryn didn't tighten or retreat. She set aside her brush, slipped beneath the covers, and turned to face Annie. “Then let's write our stories well,” she murmured. “Even if it's hard.”

“Yes. Let's.” Annie smiled, her heart warm and aching. She slid under her own blanket, the mattress creaking in the hush of the dormitory.

And in the moment that followed, their breathing slowed in rhythm, the distance between them closing—not erased, but bridged, one fragile moment at a time.

CHAPTER 22

Epiphany, the twelfth day, the day the girls would say goodbye to the Irish Rose orphanage. Vivian had counted down to it with dread and hope in equal measure, and now the moment had come.

She folded her nightgown with precise care, smoothing each crease as if it mattered. It didn't, of course. Once packed away in her carpetbag, it would wrinkle all the same. But her hands needed something to do, something steady. She placed the garment atop the few belongings she owned, shut the worn leather flaps, and tugged the buckle tight.

Beside her, Fiona gave her bag a decisive snap and grinned. "Aye, that's the last of it. We're ready, sisters."

"Ready as we'll ever be," murmured Annie, though her smile was faint, her gaze flicking toward the door as though reluctant to leave the dorm behind.

Vivian forced herself to stand tall, brushing a stray curl from her forehead. "Come along, then. Best not to linger."

The sisters lifted their carpetbags and moved in a line down the narrow staircase. The steps groaned beneath their weight, a sound Vivian had heard every morning of her life here. How strange that tomorrow, those same groans would go on without her.

The foyer opened wide below, washed in the pale light of morning. Sisters Rose, Agnes, and Clare stood waiting, their hands clasped, their smile reflecting with both pride and sorrow. A cluster of the younger children huddled near the banister, their nightcaps crooked and their faces solemn.

"There they are—our Irish Roses." Sister Agnes' melancholy tone spoke volumes. She reached for Vivian first, drawing her into an embrace. "God keep you, child. You'll make a wonderful nanny."

Vivian swallowed the lump in her throat. "I'll do my best, Sister. Thank you—for everything."

Fiona smiled as three of the younger girls clung to her skirts. "Nae, now, don't cry. You'll blotch up your sweet faces." She bent to kiss their curls, blinking fast herself.

Annie knelt to hug a girl who refused to let go of her hand. "Be brave, wee one. You'll grow taller than me before next spring."

Vivian set her carpetbag down and looked around the foyer one last time—the worn floorboards, the faint scent of bread drifting from the kitchen, and the cross above the door. All the pieces of home, pressed into her heart.

All seven girls huddled together in their cloaks, tension pressing down like the heavy winter sky. They'd gone through so much together—joys, sorrows, arguments. Bouts with Sister Catherine, and many disappointments and challenges. But a pledge to always be family. The Irish Rose Sisters.

Sister Rose stepped closer to the girls. Her dark habit rustled as she looked at each of them, her expression grave and full of love. "My girls, today you set out into the world. You have shown wisdom and courage far beyond your years, and I could not be prouder of each of you. I know the Lord has guided your steps to this moment, and He will not fail you in the days to come."

The girls straightened, as though her words were cloaks of strength laid upon their shoulders.

"As I mentioned days ago, I have something for you." From the pocket of her habit, Sister Rose drew a small stack of cards, each with The Lord's Prayer printed on it, the edges gilded. "So you will carry His words with you always, no matter how far you travel from these walls."

She moved first to Fiona, pressing a card into her hand. "Your hands will feed many, child. Remember, 'Give us this day our daily bread,' and know that your bread will be blessed."

To Isabel, she gave another card. "Your pen will serve truth, order, and law. Let 'Thy will be done on earth as it is in heaven' remind you that each word you copy can honor Him."

She turned to Cassie, offering her card. "Numbers may seem cold, but honesty and fairness shine through them. When you pray, 'Lead us not into temptation,' think of integrity in every column you tally."

For Annie, she smiled. "You will serve among silks and ribbons, perhaps in the company of the proud. Hold close, 'Forgive us our trespasses, as we forgive those who trespass against us.' Grace will be your finest garment."

Sister Rose then faced Taryn, whose chin lifted though her eyes glistened. "Your work will be tender and tireless, child. Remember, 'Deliver us from evil,' and know that every wound you bind and every tear you wipe away is His mercy in motion."

Turning to Gloria, she placed the card in her hand. "Though you'll be staying, your songs and teaching will guide those still younger than you. Let, 'Hallowed be Thy name,' be always upon your lips, in song and in example."

Finally, she reached Vivian, holding the last card for a long moment before giving it over. "Yours will carry a great responsibility, caring for little ones not your own. Pray often, 'Thy kingdom come,' and see it in the laughter, the discipline, and in the small souls you will shepherd."

Vivian's throat tightened as she accepted the card, its edges cool against her palm. Around her, the others clutched theirs like treasures, the weight of parting diminished by Sister Rose's blessing.

"My brave, wise girls," Sister Rose said, clasping her hands, "go with God. And remember— you will always be in my prayers." The words wrapped around them like a benediction, steadying them for the jingle of carriage bells that would soon follow.

Vivian clapped her hands. "Well, if we're going to fall to pieces, sisters, we might as well laugh while doing it. I hereby decree that each of you shall leave here with a title to be remembered by. Otherwise, how will I keep you straight in my head when I'm bossing my four spoiled children?"

That earned her a shaky laugh from the circle. The bells rang, bright and merry against the frosted street. Each new jingle tightened the knot in Vivian's chest. Despite the happy sound, the mood pressed down heavy, like snow-laden clouds.

Sister Agnes glanced out the window and nodded toward the approaching coach outside. "It's time. Fiona. Goodbye, my dear."

Fiona gave her a hug, and Sister Rose escorted Fiona out into the cold, but the girls followed, hot on their heels. Sister Rose remained on the top step, allowing the girls to say their special goodbyes alone.

Vivian gave her a dramatic bow. "Our Chef Supreme, ruler of broths and biscuits. May your soups never scorch, and may your puddings rise tall."

Fiona laughed through her tears. "Aye, and if you ever visit, I'll feed you so much, you'll roll away fat and happy."

"I'll hold you to that." Vivian gave Fiona one last squeeze before she climbed into the carriage. She waved from the window as it pulled away.

Moments later, the elegant Oliphant carriage swept in for Isabel. The sight of its polished brass fittings drew every girl's breath. Isabel's tears brimmed as she turned to them, especially Gloria.

Vivian took Isabel's hands. "Ah, our Duchess of Documents. Do try not to drown in ink pots."

Isabel managed a half laugh. "Aye, if I blot a page, I'll picture you wagging your finger over my shoulder."

Vivian grinned, though her throat ached. "See that you do."

Gloria rushed forward, clinging to Isabel with Mouser, the cat wriggling between them. "Aye! Don't forget us," Gloria pleaded.

Isabel cupped Gloria's cheek. "Blathers, my Little Lark! I'll never forget. And I'll come back often, Glorie—no matter how many books Lathrop, Smith & Oliphant bury me under."

The sisters joined in a tearful knot, even Vivian blinking fast against her own welling eyes, before Isabel let herself be guided into the carriage.

The Heath carriage was next, grand and imposing. Cassie turned pale.

Vivian pinched her cheek. "Our Numbers Queen, Countess of Columns—how many ledgers will you conquer before summer?"

Cassie sniffled, a small laugh breaking through. "Dozens…maybe hundreds, if Mr. Heath has his way."

"Then you'll be the wisest number cruncher in Manhattan," Vivian teased, holding her a moment longer before letting her go.

The hansom for Annie rattled in soon after, bound for the Buckingham Hotel, wheels crunching over the thin crust of snow. She shifted her bundle from one arm to the other, her face pale under her bonnet.

Vivian swept her a bow. "Behold, the Button-and-Bow Baroness! Mistress of ribbons and ruler of hems. Don't forget us when you're sewing gowns for the grandest ladies."

Annie shook her head with a grin. "I'll save you a bow, if you ever come calling."

Beside her, Taryn reached out and caught her twin's hand, holding on with a sudden, desperate grip.

"Annie," she whispered, "I swear I'll be different. I'll do better. You'll see."

Annie dropped her bundle to wrap both arms around her sister, pressing her cheek to Taryn's. "I know you will, and you've always been enough. And you'll be wonderful, Tare—those old souls won't know what hit them."

Taryn gave a shaky laugh but clung tighter. "It won't be the same without you."

Annie pulled back just enough to look her twin in the face, one so like her own. "Listen to me—I'll find a way. Manhattan or Brooklyn, hansom or no hansom, I'll come see you. You'll look up one day, and I'll be there. I promise."

For a long moment, neither moved, both trembling in the cold, bound together as though the carriages and the world could not pry them apart. Then the driver cleared his throat, and Annie had to go.

Taryn kissed her sister's cheek and whispered, "Don't forget me."

"Never," Annie said, her voice breaking. She squeezed Taryn's hand one last time before she turned and climbed into the waiting cab, leaving her twin standing in the snow, her hand still outstretched.

Then came Taryn's turn. She stood unmoving, her bag clutched tight.

Vivian touched her arm. "Our Angel of Bandages, Saint of Soup Bowls. You'll be more than a nurse—you'll be someone's hope."

Taryn blinked hard. "Don't make me cry, Viv. I'll never stop."

Vivian drew her in close. "Don't be afraid to cry, and then go do the work only you can do."

Taryn nodded, hugging her once more before stepping into the waiting cab.

Now just Gloria and Vivian remained. Gloria clutched Mouser, tears sliding down her cheeks. "You'll remember us, won't you? Promise you'll remember me and Mouser."

Vivian kissed her forehead. "Our Choir Mistress Extraordinaire, Gloria. We'll all hear your songs in our hearts, no matter where we go."

Gloria clung to her, whispering, "Aye. I'll keep on singing for you. For Him."

One by one, the wagons and coaches had come. Each arrival seemed to toll like a bell of parting. Some girls had gone with trembling eagerness, stepping up to greet those who would guide them into service. Others hesitated, glancing back at the Irish Rose Orphanage as though hoping to be called back, to be told it was all a mistake. Through it all, Vivian tried to keep her chin high, though her throat ached.

She thought of the years here—shared lessons, quarrels smoothed over, secret laughter whispered under quilts at night. And now, like beads scattering from a broken string, they were each being carried away, set apart into new households.

Her own turn would come soon. She smoothed the skirts of her plain wool gown, willing her hands not to shake. Still, she told herself, Epiphany was a day of revelation, of journeys taken and gifts brought forth. Perhaps her journey might lead to some light yet unseen.

Then came the final bells—bright, merry, and final. A gleaming black sleigh swept into the courtyard, horses tossing their heads and their breath streaming into the cold.

Vivian's heart pounded. Four children. A strict home. A nanny's assistant. Her turn had come.

She faced Gloria who braved the cold, forcing a smile. "Well, I'll be busy scolding those spoiled children, but don't think I'll ever forget you."

The last round of embraces felt fierce and tearful. Vivian's vision blurred as she climbed into the sleigh. She turned back, hand raised, watching as the orphanage, and Gloria with Mouser shrank into the snowy distance.

Only when they vanished from sight did she face forward, the ache of parting burning deep—but with the trembling hope of what lay ahead.

EPILOGUE

May 1886…Ten years later

"The Irish Rose still blooms. Not just on our necks, but in our hearts—warmed by faith, rooted in sisterhood, and watered by love."

From Annie

Dearest Sisters,

I am so grateful for our annual Round Robin letter and hope we will continue this tradition all our lives. I can scarcely believe it has already been a full year since I took up my post with the Dewey sisters after leaving the Buckingham Hotel. What began as a simple opportunity has grown into something dear to me. The girls are sweet and clever, and their household is lively with music and reading and endless little adventures. They've welcomed me with warmth, and I've come to feel at ease in their company. This summer, we shall return once again to the Thousand Islands and the Deweys' summer home on Friendly Island, and I find myself counting the days until I might see you, Vivian, Isabel, and Gloria, and perhaps by God's good grace Cassie and Fiona, my dear sisters, but especially you, Taryn.

As I mentioned last year, the sun on the water, and the faint laughter that always seems to echo across the river—all of it fills my soul with peace. We are sure to have many outings—rowing along the shoreline, picnicking among the pines, and perhaps even a dance or two under the stars.

But none of these joys would be complete without seeing some of you again. To gather together, to reminisce, to sit in silence and know we are still bound by something stronger than time or distance— that is what I long for most. And I hope the good Lord somehow brings us all together one day.

With all my heart,

Annie

From Taryn

My Irish Rose Friends,

I am excited to share that I've recently accepted a position as private duty nurse to a Civil War veteran, Mr. Henry Heath and his family, thanks to you, Cassie, referring me to them. The work is meaningful and challenging, just as I hoped it would be. I feel useful, needed, and that gives me strength. Their kindness has not gone unnoticed, either, and I'm grateful to be serving a family so gracious.

This summer, I'll accompany them to Nobby Island, which from what I've been told is very close to some of the Thousand Islands a few of you have spoken of. I hear it is serene and beautiful, so I imagine quiet mornings with birdsong and river breezes, and perhaps the occasional walk along mossy trails where the only sound is the whisper of the trees. Though I'm sure my responsibilities will keep me busy, my thoughts are already reaching toward you.

I know that you, Annie, Vivian, Isabel, and Gloria have been there in the past, and I hope to see you this summer, but I wonder—might the rest of you find your way to the Thousand Islands too? Even a short visit would mean the world. For though I am grateful for the family I serve, I do miss the conversations that sisters can have—the kind full of laughter, gentle teasing, and hearts laid bare. We have come a long way since our Irish Rose days together, and I hope we can share our lives in this season—and always.

Yours in love and loyalty,

Taryn

From Fiona

Hello, dearest girls!

Aye, if you could only see the grin on my face! I've been offered a position as assistant cook at the Westminster Park Hotel on Wellesley Island—a post I never dared dream might come my way, and I'm heading to the Thousand Islands soon. I hear that the kitchen there is grand and well run, with room for creativity and growth. I imagine pots bubbling with rich stews, trays of scones golden from the oven, and the scent of spice and sugar curling into the rafters. What excites me even more is the thought of being so close to many of you. Westminster Park is on the far eastern end of Wellesley Island, and though it is a little far from several of you (I looked it up on a map!) I still plan to watch the shoreline each day in hopes of seeing the gift of a familiar face in a rowboat gliding into view.

I know I'll be busy—meals don't prepare themselves, after all! But if you come, I'll find time, somehow, for laughter in the staff quarters, secrets traded beneath moonlight, and updates about how far we've all come. My sleeves might be rolled and my hair pinned up tight, but my heart? It's wide open and waiting for all of you.

With excitement and affection,

Fiona

From Vivian

Darling Sisters of the Irish Rose,

As I write this, the light through the parlor windows on St. Elmo Island dances across the floor in golden streaks, and little six-year-old Louis Hunt dozes on the chase lounge nearby. I've cared for him for three years now, through naptimes and long evenings, through a bout of the flu and losing his first tooth, and I can truly say the little lad has become like family to me—and so much easier than the four I had before. Though the work is constant, it is steady and rewarding, and St. Elmo Island provides a peacefulness I never knew I craved.

Annie, Taryn, Isabel, and Gloria, I do hope to see you this summer. And Taryn and Fiona, I'm thrilled that you'll get to enjoy the Thousand Islands. In case you don't know, Taryn, your Nobby Island is quite close to Friendly Island where Annie will be working and to St. Elmo where I will be. And guess what? Comfort Island, where Isabel works, is just upriver and across the channel, so perhaps we can all connect this summer, by God's merciful grace.

Wouldn't it be grand if all seven of us could get together somehow, especially here in this lovely place? The beauty of the Thousand Islands never fails to move me. St. Elmo lies nestled among its neighbors like a jewel among velvet, and from the veranda, I can see several other isles—each one holding a mystery, a promise, a memory. The distance between them seems to shrink each summer, as though the river itself conspires to bring us back together.

I think of you all often. I think of our beginnings, of where we came from, of the strength we found in one another. I hope this summer brings you near so I might hug you, hear your voices, and remind you that neither time nor tides can erase the bonds we made.

With most tender hopes,

Vivian

From Isabel

My Dearest Sisters,

It feels strange and wonderful to write to you with good news that I'll be in the Thousand Islands this summer. As you know, for two years now, I've served as the personal secretary and calligrapher to the Oliphant family. My days are filled with parchment, ink, and the most curious of correspondence. I find great pleasure in the rhythm of the work—the scratch of the pen, the beauty of a well-formed letter—and the Oliphants have come to trust me deeply.

I was fortunate to visit their summer home, Neh Mahbin on Comfort Island, last summer. Just once, but it left its mark. The place feels enchanted, as though time itself slows at the shoreline. The breeze carries music, the gardens bloom with rare flowers, and the stars—oh, the stars seem close enough to touch.

I long to return. I long to walk its winding paths again, perhaps with one of you beside me. There is something so magical about sharing a beautiful place with those who understand your heart. If any of you find yourselves nearby, like Annie, Taryn, or Vivian, know that there will be a welcome waiting. And of course, my Little Lark, my darling sister, Gloria, I will do everything in my power to see you this summer.

With ink-stained fingers,

Isabel

From Gloria

Dearest Friends and Sisters,

I miss you all so much, but I am doing well. As you know, after I left my first position, I have now served Mary Hannah Packer as her lady's maid for three years, and I've come to know her life almost better than my own.

We've spent the last two summers on Little Lehigh Island, a place in the Summerland Group of islands and unlike any other. It lies farther out than most, right on the waters of the Canadian border, but not too far from the Westminster Park Hotel, Fiona. I've been there twice and find the park and hotel very nice.

The journey from Little Lehigh can feel long—but Miss Mary often visits others on their islands nearer to you. She also plays tennis, so we visit the resorts with tennis courts several times every summer.

Annie, Taryn, Isabel, and Vivian, I do hope to see you this summer. Perhaps we will all connect at an outing or tennis event. Maybe we'll meet at a German or dance and we can sneak away and visit for a while. I pray we can.

Out on Lehigh, it's as though the world hushes and the sky feels wider. The air carries secrets, and now, I have a secret to share with you.

This year brings change. Mary has suddenly married, and with that union comes a measure of uncertainty for me. Will I remain in her service, or will I be cast aside? I do not yet know, but I cling to the comfort that the islands offer—and the strength you all inspire in me. I do hope to find encouragement in your company somehow.

Even if Little Lehigh feels distant, I'll be watching the waters, hoping for a boat carrying one of your smiles. If not in person, then in letters for your words are always a balm to me.

With steady hands and an open heart,

Gloria

From Cassie

My Sweet Sisters,

If you knew the roads I've walked these past several months after leaving Mr. Heath's employ, your hearts might ache with mine. I began my journey with hope, but I met more closed doors than open ones. Still, I refused to give up.

And now, at last, I've been offered a chance for that elusive success I seek, a bookkeeping position at the Edgewood Resort in Alexandria Bay near to so many of you. Thank you, my dearest Isabel, for your recommendation to apply for this position, and I hope and pray you will visit the resort and we will be able to see one another, and the rest of you too.

When I first heard of this opportunity, I thought only of work. But then I remembered Vivian's tales of river sunsets and Gloria's description of gentle winds and glowing lanterns. I longed for Annie's view of the St. Lawrence River and Isabel's peace. It all sounded like a place where I could begin again, not just in my career, but in spirit.

So here I am, and I'll do my utmost to prove myself, to show that I am not the girl I once was, so uncertain and timid. I am attempting to forge something new, and I hope that part of my journey includes seeing you—my sisters—once more. I want to laugh with you again, to cry if need be, and to remind ourselves that we're still blooming, even now.

I will send our precious Round Robin letter back to Annie to continue the tales of this coming year, and I hope that in it we will share our thoughts of being together—all of us—again in the Thousand Islands! Until that special moment, I continue to hope.

With all the courage I can muster,

Cassie

~ ~ ~

THE END

AUTHOR NOTES

Why set my story in a NYC orphanage?

Although the orphanage—and the orphan girls—are fictional, much research went into their creation. By the mid-to-late nineteenth century, hundreds of thousands of Irish immigrants had settled in New York, many fleeing the Great Famine. Poverty, disease, industrial accidents, and poor living conditions left many children without parents. By the 1870s, orphanages were becoming powerful institutions in NYC, serving thousands of children. They were both an act of charity and a defense of immigrant identity in a city where Irish Catholics were still marginalized. While care and conditions varied, some reports describe decent care with food, shelter, and training. Others noted overcrowding, strict discipline, and minimal care—reflecting the nineteenth-century institutional mindset. Over time, these institutions laid groundwork for schools, hospitals, and wider social services.

Why an Advent wreath?

The Advent wreath is a beloved Christian symbol that carries both ancient roots and deep meaning for the Christmas season. Its origins reach back to pre-Christian Europe, where evergreen wreaths were used during the dark winter months as signs of hope and the promise of returning light. In the sixteenth century, German Lutherans first adapted this practice for Christian devotion, and by the nineteenth century, the custom had spread widely among Protestant and Catholic communities alike. By the early twentieth century, the Advent wreath had become a familiar and cherished part of Christmas, especially in Europe and America.

The design of the wreath itself is rich in symbolism. Its circular shape represents eternity and the never-ending love of God, while the evergreen branches stand for everlasting life and faith that endures even in struggle and hardship. Four candles—traditionally three purple and one rose—are set around the wreath, each representing a different theme of the Advent journey. The first purple candle recalls the prophets and their message of hope. The second, also purple, points to the faith and peace found in Christ's coming. The third candle, rose-colored, is lit on the third Sunday of Advent and symbolizes joy as the celebration of Christmas draws near. The fourth purple candle represents love and peace, reminding Christians of the angels' proclamation of goodwill to all. In some traditions, a fifth white candle, called the Christ candle, is placed at the center and lit on Christmas Eve or Christmas Day to signify the arrival of Jesus, the Light of the World.

Beyond its symbolism, the Advent wreath plays an important role in the spiritual life of the church and the home. Lighting its candles week by week builds anticipation for the coming of Christ and helps Christians prepare their hearts during Advent.

Especially in the darkest time of the year, the Advent wreath proclaims the central truth of the season—that Jesus Christ is the true light who overcomes darkness, bringing hope, peace, joy, and love to the world.

Why an Irish Rose locket?

An Irish Rose locket serves as a profoundly meaningful and memorable symbol for the girls, especially when tied to faith and personal growth. The rose has long been a symbol of love, beauty, and resilience, while the Irish rose in particular carries layers of cultural and spiritual meaning. For the Irish, the rose is often connected to both Ireland itself, so the Irish Rose locket becomes more than a piece of jewelry—it is a keepsake that embodies faith, identity, and enduring strength.

And what about the rest of their stories?

In The Irish Rose Sisters: A Thousand Islands Gilded Age series, the Irish Rose orphans—who vowed to be "forever sisters" while at the Brooklyn's Irish Rose Orphan Asylum for Girls—find themselves reunited in the breathtaking beauty of New York's Thousand Islands ten years after departing the orphanage.

Each book follows one girl as she serves in a grand island setting, navigating the dazzling world of America's elite while confronting personal wounds from the past. Amid class divides, spiritual awakenings, and romantic challenges, these women face the unspoken expectations of their era while they hope for something more. In the midst of summer castles and sweeping river vistas, they rediscover the strength of their sisterhood, the power of love, and a deepening faith that anchors them through every trial. This series invites readers to journey through the Thousand Islands alongside these courageous heroines—whose futures prove far more golden than they ever dared dream.

Books in the series

Annie's Admission

Dewey's Friendly Island, 1886

She serves the debutantes who chase love and luxury—but what if her own heart is longing for more?

Annie Burns is content to keep her head down and her lady's maid duties in order. From lavish summer galas to riverfront picnics, Annie's job is to ensure May and Ella Dewey stay polished and proper—but lately, their flirtations and mischief are spiraling out of hand. Then, a chance encounter on the tennis court changes everything. When Martin White, a handsome young tennis buff with a keen eye for talent, mistakes her for a lady of leisure, Annie is swept into a romantic charade she never meant to start.

Encouraged by the flirtatious whims of the spirited Dewey sisters and caught between loyalty and longing, Annie must decide whether honesty will cost her the love she's only just begun to find. As her feelings for Martin deepen, Annie must battle with guilt and duty.

Can she tell him the truth without breaking his trust—and her heart? Or will the walls of class and propriety keep her from the life she longs for?

Taryn's Triumph
Nobby Island 1886
When scars run deep and secrets surface, only faith can lead them home.

Taryn Walsh never imagined she'd leave the crowded hospital in Brooklyn—until a twist of fate sent her to the remote Nobby Island. Hired as the private nurse for a battle-scarred Civil War veteran who suffers from recurring malaria, she steps into a world of soldiers, secrets, and the Thousand Island magic.
Colin Byrne, the gruff, brooding spy-turned-bodyguard—and fiercely loyal caretaker—guards more than just the island estate. Haunted by the war and carrying his own hidden scars—inside and out— Colin wants nothing more than to protect his world. But with Taryn's arrival, everything begins to shift, and he's desperate to stay in the shadows.

Trapped together in close quarters as they navigate the rhythms of island life, sparks fly in the most unexpected ways. What begins as guarded companionship slowly grows. But secrets run deep,

and when Taryn finds Colin's hidden Medal of Honor, it holds the power to shatter the secrets, and she must choose between truth and scandal.
With emotional walls crumbling and hearts on the line, will Taryn risk everything for the truth, or will echoes of the past crush their growing bond?

Fiona's Freedom
Westminster Park Hotel on Wells Island 1886 *Shame tried to silence her. Faith gave her a voice.*

Fiona King never meant to step into her mother's shoes—let alone fill them. She arrives at the grand Westminster Park Hotel on Wells Island carrying nothing but her late mother's tarnished legacy and a box of handwritten Irish recipes.

To her astonishment, instead of being a hideaway cook, she's given command of the kitchen—a position for the seasoned chef, not an insecure orphan. Overwhelmed by expectations and haunted by whispers of inadequacy, Fiona is desperate to prove herself worthy. But self-doubt is a ruthless enemy, and the pressures of perfection threaten to consume her. Then a surprise ally enters her world.

Conor McGinty, the maître d'hôtel with a disarming smile, sees past Fiona's insecurities to the talent she doesn't yet believe she has. With his steady encouragement and deep-rooted faith, Conor urges Fiona to honor her heritage—and her calling—by reviving the humble recipes that once filled her mother's kitchen with laughter, love, and warmth. As they work together, a tender friendship blossoms.

But just as Fiona begins to reclaim her God-given gifts, a *Watertown Times* scathing review that hints at her mother's scandal strikes at her deepest wounds, threatening to unravel her fragile confidence and destroy her reputation. Fiona must make a choice—cling to fear and shame or step boldly into the freedom God offers.

And what about Isabel, Gloria, Vivian, and Cassie? Stay tuned for more!

ABOUT THE AUTHOR

Susan G Mathis is an international award-winning, multi-published author of stories set in the beautiful Thousand Islands, her childhood stomping ground in upstate NY. Susan has been published more than thirty times in full-length novels, novellas, and non-fiction books and has sixteen in her fiction line. Her book awards include four Illumination Book Awards, four American Fiction Awards, three Indie Excellence Book Awards, six Literary Titan Book Awards, three Golden Scroll Awards, a Living Now Book Award, and a Selah Award.

Before Susan jumped into the fiction world, she served as the Founding Editor of *Thriving Family* magazine and the former Editor/Editorial Director of twelve Focus on the Family publications. Her first two published books were nonfiction. *Countdown for Couples: Preparing for the Adventure of Marriage* with an Indonesian and Spanish version, and *The ReMarriage Adventure: Preparing for a Life of Love and Happiness*, have helped thousands of couples prepare for marriage. Susan is also the author of two picture books, *Lexie's Adventure in Kenya* and *Princess Madison's Rainbow Adventure*. Moreover, she is published in various book compilations including five *Chicken Soup for the Soul* books, *Ready to Wed, Supporting Families Through Meaningful Ministry, The Christian Leadership Experience,* and *Spiritual Mentoring of Teens.* Susan has also written several hundred published magazine and newsletter articles. Susan is past president of American Christian Fiction Writers-CS (ACFW), former vice president of Christian Authors Network (CAN), a member of Christian Independent Publishing Association (CIPA), and a regular writer's contest judge. For over twenty years, Susan has been a speaker at writers' conferences, teachers' conventions, writing groups, and other organizational gatherings. Susan makes her home in Northern Virginia and enjoys traveling around the world but returns each summer to the Thousand Islands she loves. Visit www.SusanGMathis.com for more.

OTHER BOOKS BY SUSAN G MATHIS

Madison's Mission: A Boldt Castle story
Madison Murray, maid to Louise Boldt, harbors a singular mission—to care for her ailing mistress while hiding her own painful past. She meets Emmett O'Connor, but just as their relationship grows, tragedy shatters their world, and Madison is ensnared in a dangerous coverup. When Mrs. Boldt passes away, Madison is left reeling, can she move forward? Will Emmett forge a future alongside the woman who has captured his heart?

Love at a Lighthouse series
Join the Row-family women, Libby, Julia, and Emma, as they navigate the isolation, danger, and hope for lasting love at three Thousand Islands lighthouses—Tibbetts, Sister, and Rock Island—in the St. Lawrence River.

Libby's Lighthouse
When the Tibbett's Point Lighthouse keeper's daughter finds a mysterious sailor with amnesia, the secrets she uncovers may change her life forever.

Julia's Joy
She came to Sister Island to claim her inheritance, but the mysterious lighthouse keeper, William Dodge, makes her question all her plans.

Emma's Engagement

Rock Island lighthouse. A new wife for lightkeeper Michael Diepolder. A jealous daughter. Can love shine through the darkness?

A Summer at Thousand Island House
Addison Bell serves children of the Thousand Island House guests on Staple's Island. She meets Liam Donovan and Lt. Worthington, single father of mischievous Jimmy. When former President Chester Arthur finds Jimmy as a stowaway on his fishing boat, her job and reputation are endangered. How can she calm the churning waters of Liam, Lt. Worthington, and the President, clear her name, and avoid becoming the scorn of the community?

Mary's Moment
As the first telephone switchboard operator for the Thousand Islands Park, Mary Flynn risks her life to call for help when fire blazes through the Thousand Islands Park Commons. Widowed fireman George Flannigan takes every opportunity to connect with Mary. But they both have secrets, and when he can't stop the Columbian Hotel—and almost a hundred cottages—from being burned to the ground, Mary is left homeless. Will she be consumed by her painful past or embrace the future? Will he?

Peyton's Promise
Peyton Quinn prepares the Calumet Castle ballroom for a summer gala. As upholsterer and suffragette, when her pyrotechnics-engineer father is seriously hurt, she takes over the fireworks display despite

being socially ostracized. Patrick Taylor, Calumet's carpenter, hopes to win her heart, yet can Peyton ignore the prejudices and persevere or lose her job, forfeit Patrick's love and respect, and become the talk of local gossips?

Devyn's Dilemma

Devyn McKenna is forced to work in the Towers on Dark Island. But when Devyn finds herself in service to the wealthy Frederick Bourne family, her life takes an unexpected turn. Brice McBride, Mr. Bourne's valet, tries to help the mysterious Devyn find peace and love in her new world, but she can't seem to stay out of trouble—especially when she's accused of stealing Bourne's money for Vanderbilt's NYC subway expansion.

Katelyn's Choice

Katelyn Kavanagh finds herself in the service of none other than the famous George Pullman, and the transition proves anything but easy. Thomas O'Neill also works on Pullman Island and tries to help her adjust to her new world, but she just can't seem to tame her gossiping tongue—even when it could endanger her job, the 1872 re-election of Pullman guest President Ulysses S. Grant, and the love of the man of her dreams.

Rachel's Reunion

Rachel Kelly serves the most elite patrons at the famed New Frontenac Hotel on Round Island. When her old beau, Mitch, shows up, he opens the wound she thought was healed. As captain of a touring yacht, his attempts to win Rachel back are thwarted, especially when a wealthy patron seeks her attention. Who will Rachel choose?

Colleen's Confession

Colleen Sullivan conceals secrets when she works on Comfort Island. She loves to draw and dreams of growing in the craft, but when tragedy strikes, her orphan dreams are dashed. Jack Weiss is smitten by the lovely Irish lass. Introducing her to the famous impressionist, Alson Skinner Clark, brightens her opinion of him. But rumors of war in Europe mean Jack must choose between war and a life with Colleen. If she will have him.

Reagan's Reward

Reagan Kennedy is governess to the Bernheim's twin nephews, but her life at Cherry Island's Casa Blanca is complicated. When Daniel, the island's caretaker-boatman, tries to help the alluring Reagan, her insecurities mount as her confidence is shaken—especially when she crosses the faith divide and when Etta Damsky makes her life miserable. As trouble brews, Daniel sees another side of the woman he's come to love.

Sara's Surprise

Sara O'Neill works as an assistant pastry chef at the Thousand Islands Crossmon Hotel where she meets seven-year-old Madison and her charming father and hotel manager, Sean Graham. But Jacque LaFleur, the pastry chef, makes her dream job a nightmare. When Sean misreads Sara's desire to learn from the pastry chef as love, can Sean trust her and can Sara trust him—and can she trust herself to be an instant mother?

Christmas Charity
Susan Hawkins and Patrick O'Neill find that an arranged marriage is much harder than they think, especially when they emigrate from Wolfe Island, Canada, to Cape Vincent, New York, in 1864, just a week after they marry—with Patrick's nine-year-old daughter, Lizzy, in tow. Can twenty-three-year-old Susan Hawkins learn to love her forty-nine-year-old husband and find charity for her angry stepdaughter? With Christmas coming, she hopes so.

The Fabric of Hope: An Irish Family Legacy After struggling to accept the changes forced upon her, Margaret Hawkins and her family take a perilous journey on an 1851 immigrant ship to the New World, bringing with her an Irish family quilt she is making. A hundred and sixty years later, her great granddaughter, Maggie, searches for the family quilt after her ex-pawns it. But on their way to creating a family legacy, will these women find peace with the past and embrace hope for the future, or will they be imprisoned by fear and faithlessness?